Frances Y. McHugh

Jill Grayson, in need of a month's complete peace and quiet, rented a shack on a Maine beach, where she could eat, sleep and read murder mysteries. She had barely unlocked the door, however, before her nearest neighbor dropped by to advise her to be certain to lock it before retiring and to warn her that her life might be in danger. Jill realized uneasily that, apart from this stranger, there was nothing between her and the village but a Victorian monstrosity of a house inhabited by her landlady and her sinister birds . . .

THE FRIGHTENED BOWERBIRD

Frances Y. McHugh

Curley Publishing, Inc.
South Yarmouth, Ma.

Library of Congress Cataloging-in-Publication Data

McHugh, Frances Y.
 The frightened bowerbird / Frances Y. McHugh.
  p. cm.
 Published in large print.
 1. Large type books. I. Title.
 [PS3563.C3685F75 1991]
 813'.54—dc20
 ISBN 0–7927–0835–0 (lg. print)   90–15484
 ISBN 0–7927–0836–9 (pbk: lg. print)   CIP

Published in Large Print by arrangement with Donald MacCampbell, Inc. in the United States, Canada, the U.K. and British Commonwealth and the rest of the world market.

Distributed in Great Britain, Ireland and the Commonwealth by CHIVERS LIBRARY SERVICES LIMITED, Bath BA1 3HB, England.

Printed in Great Britain

Chapter One

The low hanging moon made an aisle of orange light across the water as I walked along the narrow duckboard that led from the roadway to the beach shack. I had rented the place at Sand's End by mail, without seeing it, and for a moment I wondered if I'd been smart to come all the way up to that isolated Maine beach alone.

But I'd had a hard year as a free lance commercial artist, working overtime, meeting deadlines and all that sort of thing, and I needed this month of peace and quiet. All I wanted was to laze in the sun, swim a little, paint what I wanted, when I wanted to, if I could generate that much ambition and energy. If I didn't, I'd just lounge around and read murder mysteries, most of them written by Peter Lindy, my favorite mystery writer.

It was going to be wonderful. No phone to ring. No messengers arriving at my studio with rush jobs. No Ed Harding demanding I marry him right away and settle down by housekeeping for him, while he raced around the world gathering material for newspaper and magazine articles – and investigations.

1

He was great on investigations. Whenever he heard something the least bit unusual was going on somewhere, he would immediately go there and rout around and find out all he could and then write it up, sometimes blowing up some infinitesimal thing to such large proportions that he often caused a lot of unnecessary trouble. This was one of the bones of contention between us, and I was glad to be able to get away from it for a while.

I liked Ed a lot, but I wasn't quite sure I loved him. So how could I say I'd marry him? And the more he tried to push me, the more I procrastinated.

The whole thing had been piling up on me for the past several months until my nerves were on the verge of shattering into shards.

Oh, well, I had this month of peace and quiet ahead of me, and I was going to enjoy it to the utmost. Now then, where was that key I'd picked up at the real estate man's house in Pine Grove Harbor? There it was, hiding behind my pack of cigarettes. With a sigh of relief, I took the key from my purse and inserted it in the lock of the door.

Then, seeming to come from nowhere, a station wagon drove up and parked behind my secondhand Falcon, and a large figure stepped out of it into the backdrop of the orange moon. I jumped nervously, then gave

2

a silly little laugh, ashamed of my lack of control. "Oh, you scared me!" I told the man who was coming toward me.

"Sorry. Are you the new tenant?" His voice was pleasant, and as he came closer I could see his face by the light of the moon. It was deeply tanned and had a rock-like ruggedness that made you know that here was a man. He had on khaki trousers and a blue shirt open at the neck, with the sleeves rolled up, exposing powerful forearms.

"Yes, I'm the new tenant, Jill Grayson. And may I ask who you are?"

"Someone you'd better be nice to."

"Oh, why?"

"Because I'm the fellow who lives in the house nearest you, and you will be dependent upon me for your fresh water supply."

I didn't like the idea of being dependent upon anybody for anything. I said, "Oh? How far away is your place?"

"Over yonder. About half a mile down the beach, across a couple of sand dunes, or about half a mile from the main road as you drive into the village. But I'm lucky enough to have a well."

I began to realize that I was all alone with this strange man with nothing closer than the village, which was at least three miles away. Unless you counted that big monstrosity of a

3

Victorian house at the very end of the village.

I asked, "What is that big, spooky-looking house just as you leave the village?"

"You must mean the old Phipps place. Woman by the name of Whitmore lives there."

"It's dark green with a lot of old-fashioned gingerbread trimmings and turrets and chimneys and things. And strange noises come from it. It's rather frightening."

The man smiled. "There really isn't anything to be frightened of. Mrs. Whitmore is a bird fancier and has a large aviary out back of the house. She has some very interesting birds. You might like to see them sometime."

"Then I suppose it was the birds I heard as I drove past. They sounded more like banshees."

The man laughed. "They are all tropical birds from New Guinea. Some of them are rather weird."

Turning the key I had put into the lock of the door, I said, "Well, thanks for telling me. And as far as the water goes, I guess I can get along without any tonight."

The man turned toward his car. Over a broad shoulder he said, "You won't have to. I've brought you a pail."

He got it from the back of his car and came into the shack with me. "I'll put it in the
4

kitchen for you," he said. Without lighting a light, he crossed what seemed to be a living room and went through a doorway to another room. I heard the pail bang down on the floor, then the sound of a striking match, which sent a glow of light in from the kitchen to where I stood.

I tossed my purse and a paperback, entitled "The Corpse on the Beach," onto a plain wooden table that was empty but for a kerosene lamp.

After a moment the man returned, struck another match and lit the lamp. Then he went into another room and lit a light in there, probably another lamp. Coming back, he said, "Now you can see your way around. And incidentally, there is no running water here. The kitchen has an old-fashioned icebox, and I believe Mr. Brown arranged for the iceman to put in a piece of ice this morning."

I looked at him and said, "Thank you. And I figured there was no running water, or you wouldn't be bringing it to me in a pail."

He grinned. "Quick on the uptake, aren't you?" he said.

"I try to be." Now I could get a better look at him, I saw his eyes were gray and his sun-streaked light brown hair was tangled from the winds of the sea. His nose and mouth were large but fitted his face perfectly. And when he smiled he showed even white teeth. "You seem to know your way around here quite well," I told him.

He said, "Yes, I do. I lived here awhile in the spring, until I could get the place I'm in now fixed up. I'm David Carter." He smiled a little, adding, "I'm a nice guy, if folks let me alone. But I'm not very sociable, especially this summer. As a matter of fact, I openly discourage visitors." He looked down at me thoughtfully for a moment, then shrugged and gave me a lopsided smile. "Thought you might as well know."

I was furious. Did he really think I could want to visit him? "You needn't worry," I assured him. "I am quite antisocial myself. At least I plan to be for the next four weeks. I may even go thirsty rather than call on you for water."

He grinned, and his whole face seemed to light up. "That would be very silly. I'll be glad to bring you a pail every day. That will do for your drinking and cooking, and you'll have to do your bathing in the ocean."

I realized he meant well, and whatever his reasons were for wanting to keep to himself, they were his own business and none of mine. So I said, "Thank you," thinking that if the situation got too sticky I could buy bottled spring water in the village for drinking and cooking.

He stood there a moment, looking down at the book on the table. Then he said, "I've often wondered who read those things." On the cover of the book was a picture of a disarranged blonde lying facing down on a beach with a knife in her back.

I couldn't help smiling. "Well, I do," I admitted. "They're relaxing."

"Relaxing?" he almost yelled. "You find violent death relaxing?"

I felt silly. "What I mean is, it gets you out of yourself. You forget your own problems."

He looked at me thoughtfully, started to say something, then seemed to change his mind. With a shrug, he walked to the door. "By the way," he said, "there are some of my clothes in the bedroom closet. I'll bring over a suitcase some day and get them out of your way."

I followed him to the door. "All right. And thanks for the water."

"It was a pleasure." Then, as an afterthought, "Be sure your front and back doors are locked when you go to bed."

He was halfway to his car as I called, "For goodness sakes, why?"

He got into the car, closed the door, then, sticking his head out of the window, yelled,

"As a special favor to me." Then he turned the car around and sped off, leaving me standing in the doorway.

Chapter Two

The next morning, after a swim and breakfast on the tiny back porch, I took my easel and a freshly stretched canvas, together with my paint box and a folding camp stool, and went down the beach. I hoped my neighbor wouldn't come over while I was painting, because I hated to have anyone watch me when I was working.

It wasn't until the sun was high in the sky, changing the light so I had to stop work, that I saw a girl coming up the beach toward me.

When she reached me I started to smile, but the girl asked, rather unpleasantly, "What are *you* doing here?" She was a pretty girl, even though her nose was rather flat and her lips a bit too thick. Her hair was short, curly and black, and her eyes were large, intelligent and a bright blue – a startling contrast. I guessed her to be about my age – twenty-two. She was wearing a colorful cotton shift that stopped just above her extremely

8

pretty coffee-colored knees. When she spoke she had a slight British accent.

I began to pick up my things. "I came out here to paint," I told her. "I didn't think there would be anyone around."

The girl gave me a skeptical look. Then, glancing at my painting, she said, "Not bad. You've caught the feeling of the dunes jolly well." Then, in a brisker tone, "Just see to it that you stick to your painting." With that cryptic remark she turned and walked back in the direction from which she'd come, toward David Carter's house.

The afternoon was hot, so I stayed inside the shack and read for a while. "The Corpse on the Beach" had a locale such as the one where I was, and it lent credence to the story. At one especially exciting point, I found myself looking out the window to be sure there was no real corpse on my beach.

Then I chuckled to myself and closed the book. When I reached that point, it was time to stop reading about "violent death," as David had described it, and do something else.

Well, what was there to do? I could paint. So I began to paint a small portrait of David, from memory. It was just a sketch, but when I finished it I decided it wasn't too bad. It was nearly five o'clock, and I was putting on the last dabs of paint when I heard a car stop and footsteps on the duckboard to the front porch. The door was open, but the screen door was hooked from the inside. Fortunately my painting was facing the other way, because David peeked in at the same time as he knocked and called, "Hi there, I've brought you water."

Embarrassed because he had caught me doing a picture of him, even though he couldn't see it from where he was, I said, "I don't want it. Go away."

He looked surprised, and for a moment I thought he was going to do just that. Then he seemed to change his mind. "I'll need the empty pail you have," he said.

So I put down my brush and went and unhooked the screen door for him, and he took the pail of water into the kitchen, returning with the pail I had emptied.

On his way to the door, David stopped and looked at me. "Enjoying yourself?" he asked.

I said, "When I'm *alone*, I enjoy myself very well." That, I decided, should show him he wasn't the only one who could be antisocial.

He smiled and shrugged. "Well, as far as I'm concerned, I'd just as soon this shack had stayed unoccupied all summer. As a matter of fact, if I'd had any idea the real estate agent was going to rent it, I'd have paid the rent on it myself, just to be on the safe side."

I wiped my brush on a paint rag. "Then I'm glad you didn't know," I told him, "because I like it here." Then I asked, "Who owns the place?"

"Mrs. Whitmore."

"The one with the weird birds?"

"The same. She also used to own the place I have now, but I bought it from her." He grinned. "It's more comfortable than this – and I like to be comfortable." He came over and looked at my painting of him. Then he glanced questioningly at me, and I felt my face flush. Hastily I said, "I like to paint people from memory." I felt very foolish.

He smiled. "I'm flattered." Then he turned, and with the empty pail dangling from one hand, walked out of the shack, closing the screen door quietly after him.

Chapter Three

That evening David returned. This time he had walked along the beach, and I thought he looked worried. He said, "I know I told you I was antisocial, but I thought I'd come over for a while. Do you mind?"

"Not at all. Won't you come in?"

We sat in the cushioned wicker chairs which were all the room had to offer. "So you're an artist?" he said, nodding toward his portrait still on the easel and the partly finished canvas of the dunes, propped against the wall.

"Thanks for the compliment."

"I'm not an authority," David said, "but I'd say you are pretty good. You've caught a likeness of me that is remarkable."

I said, "Thanks again. and what do *you* do, when you're not carrying water to your neighbors?"

He grinned. "Well, I seem to be a sort of beachcomber, don't I?"

I had on rather tight blue jeans and espadrilles, an old sports shirt of Ed's that he had given me to paint in, and my face was burning from the touch of new sun I'd gotten that morning. Or was it burning because of David's intent gaze?

His gray eyes were holding mine, which happen to be a sort of amber, as if he were waiting to see if I'd accept his suggestion that he might be a beachcomber.

I decided to go along with the gag. I asked, "If you *are* a beachcomber, *why* are you?"

He shrugged. "Things happen."

12

"One doesn't have to accept things without fighting back."

He kept looking at me. His nicely shaped eyebrows rose, and the corners of his large, firm mouth turned down.

"We each have to work out our own destiny." So he wasn't going to tell me what he really did. Okay.

I said, "Very true." To my consternation, I was beginning to wonder if this man was *my* destiny. Surely he was having a strange effect on me.

Suddenly he made a quick movement and leaned forward in his chair. "Look, little lady," he said, "I wish you'd get out of here. You're in the way."

"In the way of *what?*"

I can't tell you. But if you stay here, you may be in danger."

I managed a smile. "You mean I may end up as a corpse on the beach?"

I was joking, of course, but when he answered me it was very plain *he* was *not*. "Even that," he said quietly.

I stood up, and he did the same. "Is that a threat?" I asked, my heart beating very fast.

"It's a warning."

I faced him, angry now. "Sorry," I said, "but I don't scare easily. And I am staying here for a whole month."

13

His brow puckered into a frown, and he looked annoyed. "But you mustn't," he argued. "You – well, it's not safe for a girl to stay in an isolated place like this all alone. Brown had no right to rent you the place." He approached me, and strangely, I felt myself sway toward him. "I'm not afraid of *you*, David Carter, if that's what you mean."

He smiled a little at that. "Maybe you should be." And the next thing I knew, I was in his arms, and our lips were clinging, and a dizzy ecstasy was sweeping through me. I'd never in my life experienced such an exquisite feeling. I closed my eyes and stood quietly, my body close to his, our hearts beating in unison. I could hear the swishing of the incoming tide, and I knew that forever after, when I heard an incoming tide anywhere in the world, I would remember that moment. And somewhere in the back of my head I could hear a small, warning voice saying, "You can never marry Ed Harding after this."

When at last David's arms relaxed and let me go, my common sense returned with a rush. I backed away from him, and I knew my amber eyes must be wide with the wonder of what had happened.

David said, "I'm sorry, Jill. I had no right to do that."

"Please go," I said. The words sounded more like a gulp than words, but he obeyed me. Walking to the back door, he said, "I meant what I said, Jill. I wish you wouldn't stay here. I'll reimburse you for whatever you have paid for the months' rent if you will go."

My chin went up defiantly. "Well, I shan't go!" I told him.

Reaching the door, he turned, and our eyes met head on, in a challenge I couldn't ignore. "You are going to make it very hard for me," he said.

I shrugged. "Sorry."

"And by the way, when you swim, keep away from the rocks. There is a very strong undertow around them."

"Is that another attempt to scare me away?"

"No." He stood looking at me for a moment. Then he went out, and I watched him walking along the beach, his head thrown back as if to meet the wind, his big hands rammed into the pockets of his khaki trousers.

After he was out of sight, I wrestled with the idea of following his advice. I wasn't going to be scared away so easily. However, I did lock the doors when I went to bed, also the windows, with the exception of the one in the bedroom. I had to have *some* air, and there was the screen.

15

The next thing I knew, the sun was shining in my window.

As I had my breakfast, I decided I'd pay Mr. David Carter a visit. I could take back his pail as an excuse.

I put on a new blue denim dress with big pink patch pockets made to look like tulips, tied back my auburn hair with a narrow blue ribbon, got into my car and drove over to David's. But when I arrived at his home, which was even farther from the main road than he'd said, I discovered it was a rather pretentious house, for a beach house, and it was all closed up. The shutters over the windows were hooked from the inside and the front, and the back doors were closed and locked. For the first time I really began to have doubts about David Carter. Surely he was no beachcomber if he lived in a house that size.

Wandering around, I saw there was a two-car garage at the side, and it was empty. So David and his visitor were out. The place was well kept, and there was a flower garden in the front of the house where special soil had been brought and put over the sand.

Back in my car, I drove down the sandy road toward the town of Pine Grove Harbor. I decided I'd ask a few questions about David Carter. But when I came to Mrs. Whitmore's monstrosity of a house and heard the screeching of the birds, I stopped. Curiosity was going to delay my arrival in town. As I sat in my car listening to the birds, I wondered if I dared go up to the house and ask if I might see the aviary. As I was sitting there trying to make up my mind, a tall, slender woman in navy slacks and a man's white shirt came around from the back of the house. As she came closer, I could see her face. It had the leathery, tanned look that goes with outdoor living. It was hard to believe she had ever been pretty, even when she was younger, but now she was striking-looking. I guessed her to be in her fifties. Her iron gray hair was cut short like a man's. The surprising thing about her was a pair of large hoop earrings of dull gold. As she walked, they danced beside her weatherworn face and looked incongruous.

On impulse, I got out of my car and went to meet her. "Mrs. Whitmore?" I asked.

She said, "Yes." Her eyes were large and a very dark brown.

I said, "I hope you will forgive my intrusion. I'm Jill Grayson, I've rented your beach shack out at Sand's End, and David Carter tells me you have some interesting birds here."

Her lips curved into a very small smile. "Yes, I have. Would you care to see them?"

17

I said, "Yes, I'd like to very much."

She turned and started toward the back of the house. "They're out back. If you will follow me."

I did, and when we reached the aviary I was too dumbfounded to speak. I'd never seen anything like it, except in a big zoo. It seemed as if at least an acre were fenced in with a kind of chicken wire around whatever vegetation nature had put there; trees, bushes and flowers had been enclosed for the private use of the birds. There was also a chicken wire covering over the top, in sections, about fifteen feet from the ground, giving the birds space to fly, but of course not as much as they had had in their natural habitat. The enclosure alone must have cost a considerable sum.

I said, "It's beautiful. But what happens to the birds in the winter?"

"There is an aviary down in Florida that I'm trying to buy, if I can afford it. If I can get it, I will take them there for the winter. If not –" she shrugged – "I'll have to give them to various zoos."

All I could say was, "Oh," because it was easy to see that having to part with the birds would break her heart.

She began to tell me about the birds. "They are all from New Guinea," she explained.

Then, pointing, "Those soft grey ones with the long forked tails and large white mustachios are tree-swifts."

"They are beautiful," I said.

She pointed to what looked like a pile of leaves over at one side. "That is the house of the rail," she said. "There are two of them in it. They always travel in pairs. They are very rare specimens of the little red mountain rail. We had quite a time capturing them. As I said, they go around in pairs and make those little leaf shelters to sleep in at night."

I said, "Interesting."

"You know there are several species of birds of paradise," Mrs. Whitmore went on. It was easy to see these birds were her whole life. She was devoted to them, and once she started talking about them there was no stopping her. But I didn't mind; I'd never before seen such rare specimens of bird life, and I was fascinated.

"That one over there," she said, indicating a bird about the size of a starling, "I love him as dearly as if he were a person."

The one she meant was all black with an enormous bifurcated shield of metallic greeny-blue feathers that rose from his head and swept back over his back. Another shield of metallic feathers was on his breast. "When the male displays to the female," Mrs.

19

Whitmore explained, "both those shields are erected and stand up about his head, so his face and bill are in the center of what looks like a continuous saucer-like ring."

I could only nod. I was too overwhelmed to speak.

"That bird over there," Mrs. Whitmore went on, "is the sicklebill. See – that big one. His tail is nearly three feet long. You'll notice he is a soft velvety-black all over, with the exception of those two butterfly-wing shields rising from each side of his breast."

"He has a very long bill," I commented.

She nodded. "It is about three and a half inches long. Noticed how thin and curved it is." The bird gave a loud penetrating whistle, and I almost held my ears.

There were too many specimens for my hostess to be able to describe them all to me, but I couldn't help asking about a strange-looking structure of twigs set near the front and to the side. It was shaped like a wigwam and was about three feet tall and five feet at the base. There was a rounded opening about a foot high that led into an inner chamber. In front of this curious structure was an area that looked as if it had been swept, and there was the impression of a front lawn with several small beds of flowers. I just had to ask, "What is that over there?"

"That is the house of a bowerbird," Mrs. Whitmore explained. "See; there he is coming out the door."

What I saw was a bird that looked like a fat thrush, only with blue feathers instead of brown. He had stout legs and stood there looking around as if he were proud of his home.

Mrs. Whitmore said, "There are a number of kinds of bowerbirds. Some are brown; some have brilliant plumage. This happens to be what they call a blue satin bowerbird. Would you believe he is a cousin to the birds of paradise? He builds that bower for the female. And he brings fresh flowers every day and discards the withered ones."

"How interesting. And he really brings fresh flowers for his ladylove every day?"

"Every day."

I laughed. "He is more attentive than his human counterparts."

Mrs. Whitmore smiled. "Oh, quite." She turned away from the aviary, and I knew my conducted tour was over. As we walked back toward my car, she said, "You mentioned David Carter. Is he a friend of yours?"

Hastily I said, "Oh, no. I just met him a couple of days ago; the night I arrived, as a matter of fact. He was kind enough to bring me a pail of fresh water."

She said, "That's good. I guess Mr. Brown asked him to." Then, "David is the salt of the earth, but I'd better warn you: he has no time for girls at present."

Surprised, I said, "But I saw a pretty dark-haired girl on the beach yesterday. She came from the direction of his place."

Mrs. Whitmore's face seemed to change; to become a mask. "She could have been," she said. "That was Coral. She's my granddaughter."

I said, "Oh. I she – that is, I mean – is she David's wife?"

Mrs. Whitmore made a sound that could have been interpreted as a grunt. "No," she said.

We had reached my car by then, and there was nothing for me to do but say, "Well, thank you for showing me your lovely birds. I hope I haven't bothered you."

She ran a strong browned hand through her short iron gray hair, and a large diamond ring on the third finger of her left hand sparkled as the sun struck it. "Not at all," she said. "I enjoy showing off my pets."

I said, "I can understand that. And I hope you get the aviary down in Florida."

Grimly she replied, "If I don't, it will be a very great tragedy."

I got into my car, and she stood and waited

22

for me to be seated and start the motor. Then she said, "Take a little tip from an old woman – keep out of Coral's way. She's my granddaughter, but she's not too fond of women."

I waited for her to enlarge on that, but she didn't. "Goodbye," she said, "I hope you enjoy your stay at Sand's End. If there is anything you need, just tell Mr. Brown, my real estate agent. By the way, he tells me you are a friend of Ed Harding, the news writer."

Surprised, I said, "Yes, I am."

She gave me a searching look. "I hope he isn't going to be visiting you up here."

I raised my brows, angry at the insinuation. "Not as far as I know," I told her.

She shrugged. "My reason for asking is that he has a reputation for snooping, and we don't like snoopers up here." She bowed and walked away.

It was a definite dismissal and a not too polite hint not to bother her again. I called after her, "Goodbye," and put the car in motion.

I drove down the sandy road toward the village, more determined than ever to ask some questions about David Carter. My first stop was Mr. Brown's real estate office, which was in his house. He said, "Well, good

23

morning, Miss Grayson. How are things out at Sand's End?"

"That's what I'd like to talk to you about. What kind of a man is David Carter?"

Mr. Brown, fat, squat and balding, seemed surprised. "Why, he's a very nice fellow. Behaves himself. Keeps to himself pretty much. But we never bother folks around here if they want to be left alone."

"Who is Mrs. Whitmore?"

"Well, she's a native, you might say. Born and brought up here. Owns about half the town. Inherited it from her father, old Cy Phipps. She got married late in life to a fellow who was one of those, what do you call them? – ornithologists? They used to travel a lot. Stayed here from time to time, but lived mostly in the South Seas and places like that. Then last year he died over there, and this spring she came back with a lot of queer birds. She has what she calls an aviary out back of the house."

"Yes. I've just seen it."

"Interesting, if you like that sort of thing."

"And her granddaughter?"

He shrugged. "Strange sort of girl. Grew up in one of them foreign places. She's Mrs. Whitmore's step-granddaughter. Mr. Whitmore had been married before, and Coral is the daughter of his son by his first marriage.

24

Story goes she's a half-breed. Her mother is a native of one of them South Pacific places."

"And Mr. Whitmore?"

"He was English or Canadian or something like that."

I said, "Oh." Then I asked, "Is she married? Coral, I mean?"

"Not that I know of. She never lived here until this summer. Whenever Mr. and Mrs. Whitmore came back here, they always came alone."

"Coral lives with her grandmother?"

He gave me a surprised look. "Of course. Where else would she live?"

"I was just wondering. The only time I ever saw her she came over the beach from and went back toward David Carter's place."

Mr. Brown lit a cigar and puffed on it a moment. "She won't get far with him. He don't bother with girls."

I don't know why this made me feel good, but it did. I said, "He is all right, though, as a neighbor?"

"Don't see why he wouldn't be."

I looked down at my car keys, which I was fingering nervously. "I was just wondering."

Mr. Brown got up and walked to the door with me. "You don't have to worry about David Carter," he assured me. "As a matter of fact, you're darned lucky to have such a

25

nice neighbor. You could do a lot worse. We get some characters up here in the summer sometimes."

"Yes, I suppose you do. Well, thank you." Then foolishly I asked, "Is *he* married?"

Mr. Brown smiled. "Not as far as I know." Then I remembered what Mrs. Whitmore had said about Ed Harding. "By the way, why did you tell Mrs. Whitmore I knew Ed Harding?"

He shrugged. "Didn't think it was a secret. You have him as a reference."

Leaving him, I stopped in the self-service general store for some groceries and bottles of spring water.

I decided to have lunch in the quaint little tearoom on the main floor of the Pine Grove Harbor Inn. As soon as I was seated, I saw Coral and David at a table in a far corner. David had his back to the room, and Coral was too busy talking to notice me. David kept shaking his head no to everything she said. My heart gave a queer flutter, and I lowered my head over the menu, hoping they wouldn't see me. They didn't. Just a few minutes after I came in they left, too absorbed in one another to notice that anyone else was in the room. I gave my order listlessly. So that was the way the cracker was crumbling? So David was too busy to bother with girls? So he was antisocial, was he? I couldn't help wondering if he had ever kissed Coral the way he had kissed me. I'd never realized I could be jealous. But I did wish Coral didn't look so attractive. She had on a bright red A-line dress, red flat-heeled shoes, and she was carrying a straw purse.

I've never been able to remember what I had for lunch, but afterward I went to the town's only movie and sat through an old Bob Hope-Bing Crosby film.

It was after five by the time the movie was out, and it was still quite warm. As I was driving back to the beach, I decided to have a swim as soon as I got back and had put away my groceries. I was glad to have the block of ice.

The prospect of my swim made me step on the gas. It was going to be wonderful to plunge into the tangy, cold salt water and battle the waves for a while, then lic on the sand just outside my door and relax before I had my dinner.

I was driving along, daydreaming about how nice it was all going to be, and didn't notice the blue coupé approaching until it was almost on top of me. It was coming at a breakneck speed, and I had to swerve quickly to avoid being sideswiped by it.

Annoyed by such careless driving, I made it a point to get a good look at the man at the

27

wheel as the car passed me. He had a flat sort of face, with a scar on his left cheek. His eyes, which met mine for the fraction of a second, were dark, and I thought I detected in them a look of animosity. His hair was dark and rather in need of a trim, and his lips were thick, with the lower one protruding just a trifle. It was the kind of a face you might expect to see on the front page of a tabloid newspaper.

I couldn't help wondering where he was coming from. I'd already passed the turn-off to David's house. That meant he must have been out to my place. I didn't much like the idea. But maybe he was just a salesman of some sort. They seemed to be able to find prospective customers, no matter how isolated.

I dismissed the thought of him as I neared my shack and saw it standing peacefully in the late afternoon sun.

Parking my car in front of the shack, I got out and, gathering together my bags of groceries, ran up the two steps to the porch and went inside. I'd left the place open, not dreaming that anyone would come way out there in broad daylight, unless it was David. And I didn't feel I had to bar the door to him.

Then I saw the note! It was on the plain wooden table, and it was pinned to it by an ugly-looking knife. Without touching it, I looked at the note more carefully. It was headed by a drawing of a skull and crossbones. And it read:

Get rid of the dame! If you don't, I'll come back and eliminate her myself.

There was no signature.

I was standing there staring at the note and the knife, with cold chills of fear creeping up and down my spine, when I heard steps on the back porch. My heart stopped beating; I'd never been so scared in my life. Then I heard David ask, "Anybody home?"

"Yes, come in." I almost ran to the screen door to meet him. "Oh, I'm so glad to see you!" I cried, momentarily forgetting his lunch with Coral. "Somebody was here while I was out this afternoon and left this note." I pointed to the note, stabbed to the table by the knife.

David put down the pail of water he was carrying, came over and read the note. Watching his face, I couldn't tell what he was thinking. Then he looked up at me. "You haven't touched this?"

I shook my head.

"Anything stolen?"

"I don't think so. I'll look." Hurriedly

29

I checked my belongings. Everything was as I'd left it. "No," I told him. "But I don't have anything with me that is valuable enough to steal."

He took the pail of water into the kitchen and came back with the empty one. "Mind if I see if all my clothes are there?" he asked.

"No, of course not."

He went into the bedroom and looked into the closet where his few clothes were hanging beside mine. When he came back, he said, "You can't stay here another night alone."

I stared at him. "What do you suppose the note means? Who is the dame? Surely not me?"

He raised an eyebrow comically. "Why not you?"

I was shaking now, my nerves completely on edge. "But *who* is supposed to get rid of me?"

He began to smile. "Perhaps *me*."

I kept staring at him. "I can't believe it. You seem so nice."

He was watching my face thoughtfully, all his playfulness gone. "You don't know anything about me."

"Couldn't I stay at your place tonight?"

His face clouded. "Definitely not! You'd better drive into the village and stay at the inn tonight. Then either finish your vacation there, or go back home, or some other place far away from here."

"What's the matter? Wouldn't Coral like it if I came over and stayed with you?"

He gave me a startled look. "When did you see *her?*"

"Yesterday." I decided not to let him know I'd seen them at the inn, lunching together. "She wandered onto my territory, gave me a lukewarm compliment about my painting, warned me to stick to it, then went away over toward your place."

"She probably heard you were here and came over to have a look."

"To see if I was competition?"

He smiled slightly. "Possibly."

I ignored that, asking, "Shouldn't the police be told about this threatening note?"

He said, "No," took out a handkerchief, pulled the knife from the table, wrapped it carefully in his handkerchief and placed it in the empty pail. Then he picked up the note by the corner and laid it on top of the handkerchief-wrapped knife. "And don't tell your friend Ed Harding about it," he said.

I caught my breath. "So *you* know, too?"

"I do now. I didn't when I kissed you last night."

"Perhaps I'd better set you straight. Ed

31

Harding and I are just good friends."

He gave me a steady look. "I should think having him for a friend would be precarious, if not downright dangerous."

"What do you mean by that?"

He shrugged. "Nothing is sacred with him, is it? By that I mean he has a wide-spread reputation for hearing everything, seeing everything – and telling everything."

"That's a catty remark for a man to make about another man."

He smiled ruefully. "Sorry. You're right. But – well, he did me a bad turn one time, and I'd rather not come into contact with him again."

I said, "Don't worry. You won't. He is out of the country at the moment." Then, to change the subject, I motioned to the knife. "Are you going to play detective yourself?" I asked, I guess rather sarcastically.

He got angry. "Look!" he snapped. "Will you please go away and mind your own business? You and your Ed Harding!"

I met his angry eyes defiantly. "No! I won't go away. And Ed Harding isn't here, so just leave him out of it. However, I *am* going to drive into town and tell the police about this note, because I know who wrote it. He passed me on the road in a blue coupé just now, as I was driving home from the village."

"Just *now?*" David yelled.

I nodded.

He came to me and put his hands on my shoulders and looked down into my face. "Look, Jill," he said, his anger changing to pleading. "If anything happens to you, I'd never forgive myself. You're too sweet to get mixed up in trouble." Then for the second time he took me into his arms, and his lips sought mine, and in spite of myself I gave my lips to him.

For a long blissful moment we clung together. Then he let me go. "That was for goodbye," he said, "And my apologies to Ed Harding. Now I have to get back to my place."

He turned to go, but I grabbed his arm. "David, take me with you! Don't leave me here alone! What *are* you, anyway? A coward? A crook? What?"

He pushed me away from him. "I'm sorry, Jill. I wish you hadn't come here. And for heaven's sake go home! You're making a nuisance of yourself!"

"I'm making a nuisance of myself?" I cried. "*I* am? All *I'm* trying to do is to have four weeks of peace and quiet. But what am I getting? I ask you. Whatever it is, I'm sick and tired of it! And don't bother to bring me any more water. I'll buy it in bottles in the

33

village. As a matter of fact, I bought some this afternoon."

"Okay!" he said. "But don't say I didn't warn you."

Chapter Four

In the morning when I got up, it was raining. There was a cold damp wind blowing in from the sea. I dressed quickly. No swim this morning. Before I got my breakfast, I glanced out the living room window facing the beach. I'd meant only to see how hard it was raining, but there was something on the beach that made me do a double take. It looked like a girl, lying on her face on the wet sand, the rain soaking her. And there was a knife in her back, but a different kind of knife from the one that had pinned the threatening note to the table. This looked more like a dagger. Blood had escaped from the wound and ran down on the sand, but the rain was washing it away.

Trembling, I unlocked the door, unhooked the screen, ran down the steps of the tiny porch and across the few yards of sand to where the body lay. I scrunched down on

34

my heels and tried to see the girl's face. It was pushed into the sand, and I had to touch her, turn her a little, before I could see her face. I knew I shouldn't touch her, but I had to. I had to see who she was. When I saw, I gasped. It was Coral Whitmore! This morning she was wearing a dark blue tailored dress with a white collar.

Disregarding the rain pouring down on us both, I sat down on the sand beside the dead girl. I was too shocked to move, too shocked to scream. The rhythmic swish of the oncoming tide was like a lullaby. But with every swish the waves came in closer. It would be only a matter of minutes before it reached us – me, a live girl, and Coral, a dead one. *I* could get up and run away. But Coral couldn't. And I couldn't just leave her lying there to be covered by the sea. I had to pull her up higher on the beach where the water couldn't reach her.

I looked around. There was no one in sight, and the sand dunes were nearly lost in the mist rolling in from the sea, along with the waves. If I only had a phone! Could I make the village in my car and get back with help before the waves reached the corpse? I realized there wasn't a chance. I would have to pull her to safety myself. Then and then only could I go for help.

I got up and tried to pull her by getting my hands beneath her arms at her armpits. In that way I could keep her face up so it wouldn't drag along the sand. Or that was what I thought. I hadn't reckoned with the fact that her head would flop forward like that of a rag doll without enough stuffing in its neck. And I couldn't turn her over on her back because of the knife. And I certainly couldn't pull out the knife. The very thought of touching it filled me with horror.

Swish! Swish! Swish! Each time the incoming waves came closer. I would have to hurry or they would be sweeping over us.

How long it took me to drag the body of the dead girl up to where the waves couldn't reach her could never be counted by minutes. To me it was an agonizing lifetime. But at last I succeeded. To be extra sure, I allowed for an unusually high tide because of the storm and pulled my burden up close to the shack. Then and only then did I dare leave her and go for help.

I staggered into the shack, my back aching, my arms feeling as if they had been pulled from their sockets. Shaking from head to foot, I tore off my wet clothes, put on dry ones, sneakers, my raincoat, and a weatherproof scarf over my hair, which I had tried to rub dry with a towel. Then I ran out to my car.

I didn't bother to lock up the house. What was the use?

As I drove along the wet slippery road, I wondered to whom I should go first. The police station, I supposed, was the logical place to go. But the murdered girl was Mrs. Whitmore's granddaughter. Shouldn't she be the first one to be told?

But how could I drive up to the woman's house, ask to see her, and announce, "I'm sorry, Mrs. Whitmore, but your granddaughter has been murdered. She is lying on the wet sand in back of my shack with a knife in her back."

My decision was made for me as I approached the monstrosity known as the Whitmore place. Mrs. Whitmore was standing on the front porch. She had on a raincoat, high rubber boots and an old cap pulled over her short hair. She had probably been out to the aviary, because the boots and her coat and cap were wet.

She saw my car coming along the road, came down from the porch, walked across the front lawn to the road and stood and waited for me. So what could I do but stop? I rolled down the window on her side, and she said, "Good morning. Not very good beach weather, is it?" Now I was close to her, I could see she had on the big gold hoop earrings, which looked ridiculous with the rest of her outfit.

I said, "No. But I had to come and –"

Not giving me a chance to finish, she said, "My poor birds are so bedraggled. All except the bowerbirds. They are snug in their pretty bower."

I said, "Yes. Well, I'm sorry, Mrs. Whitmore, but I have some bad news for you."

"Bad news for *me?* Has your house been washed away?"

I gulped. "No – but – that is – Coral, your granddaughter –"

She smiled brightly. "Lucky Coral," she said. "She left last night for Boston, and it isn't raining down there."

I stared at her, my mouth hanging open. "Are you sure? That is, how do you know she is in Boston?"

She looked at me as if she thought I was a little touched in the head. "How do I know she is in Boston? Because I just talked to her on the phone. She is staying with friends, and she called me." Our eyes met, and I'm sure there was fright in mine. But in hers there was nothing. And I mean that literally. They were as blank as if she were blind and couldn't see.

I was shaking from head to foot, still cold from my drenching and my horrible experience. I didn't believe I would ever get warm again. My shaking, ice cold hand reached out and managed to turn the key in the ignition, and my numb foot trod on the starter. The car sprang to life, eager to get going, as I was. To Mrs. Whitmore I said, "Well, I guess your granddaughter was smart to get away last night." What else could I say?

She said, "I'll tell her you were asking for her. Is there any message?" I noticed life was returning to the woman's eyes.

I said, "No, no message," and started the car, with a wave of my hand to the step-grandmother of the dead girl.

As I drove down the Main Street in Pine Harbor, I was in a state of shock and would have liked just to keep on driving – right on down to New York and my safe, secure studio on East 10th Street. But I couldn't just go off and leave that dead girl lying on the beach in the rain. It was merely common decency to stop and tell the police so they could do something about her.

When I did tell the police, the man at the desk said, "We'll go right out. Do you know who she is?"

I said, "Yes. She is Coral Whitmore."

"Oh, my God!" he exploded. "I'd better call old lady Whitmore."

He reached for the phone on his desk, but

I stopped him. "No, don't!" I said. "I've just seen her, and she says her granddaughter left for Boston last night."

"She must have been waylaid."

"No. Mrs. Whitmore said she talked to her on the phone a little while ago, and she was in Boston with friends."

The man, tall, broad-shouldered, about forty-five, with graying black hair and piercing black eyes, said, "Then obviously the dame on the beach isn't Coral Whitmore."

"But I am sure she is!"

The man stood up and reached for his hat, which was on his desk. "Let's go see." He went to the door of another room. "Kelly," he called, "I'm going out to Sand's End. Come on. I may need you."

In a moment, a big, redheaded man of about thirty-five came out of the room and joined us. "Sergeant Kelly," the older man introduced him. "I'm Lieutenant Cory." Again he went to the door of the other room. "Jake, come out here and take the desk," he called.

When we went out to the street, Lieutenant Cory said, "We'll go ahead. You follow us."

They drove quite fast and reached Sand's End several minutes before I did. Without waiting for me, they jumped out of their car and ran around the shack to the beach. I could see them, because the road was perfectly straight. By the time I joined them they were wandering around the shack, examining the sand. "Where did you leave the body?" Lieutenant Cory asked me.

"Up close to the shack, on the ocean side."

"There isn't anything there."

I stared at him. "There *must* be!" I ran around to the beach, and the two men followed me. The tide had come up several feet since I'd left, well past where I'd found the body, but yards away from where I'd left it. But the body was gone. There wasn't a trace of it. And the drag marks in the sand, which had been made by the body as I pulled it away from the reaching waves, had been smoothed out. There wasn't a drop of blood anywhere, either.

It had stopped raining, and the sun was trying to break through the clouds. The rocks were shining in their dark ruggedness, and the sea had little bursting whitecaps as far out as you could see.

"It was right here," I told Lieutenant Cory.

He scratched the back of his head, pushing his hat over his eyebrows. "No sign of anything having been here," he said. "You're sure?"

"Of course I'm sure!"

41

He put his hat back in place. "Let's have a look inside."

I led the way, and the two men followed me. We searched the place, which didn't take long. There was no sign of anything. My wet clothes still lay in a heap on the bedroom floor where I'd left them.

Searching the clothes closet, Lieutenant Cory asked, "Whose clothes are these?" indicating David's things.

"David Carter's. He rented the shack in the spring, he tells me. He left those things."

"Why?"

"I haven't the faintest idea."

"Did you know him before you came up here?"

"I did not."

He shut the closet door, and the three of us went into the living room. I wanted to tell him about the note I'd found yesterday, fastened to the table by the knife, but David hadn't wanted the police to know about it, and for some crazy reason I didn't want to go against David's wishes. Maybe he was a criminal – a murderer, even, but – well, anyway, I kept still about the note.

Lieutenant Cory said, "You thought the girl was Coral Whitmore?"

"I'm sure she was."

"Then what happened to her?"

I just looked at him. What was the use answering such a silly question?

"You're sure she was dead?" he asked.

"Quite dead."

The two policemen went outside and walked around the shack a couple of more times, and I followed them. There wasn't a clue of any kind. It was the second time around that I saw the small metal box laying beside the outhouse. Beside the box was a small shovel, the kind children use for playing in the sand. A few inches away was a hole, just big enough for the box. I called to Lieutenant Cory. "Look!"

He came over to where I was standing. "What's that?" he asked.

"Looks like a metal box, the kind people use to keep valuables in a safe."

Lieutenant Cory leaned down and picked it up by a corner of the lid, which was open. Examining it, he said, "Um." Then he looked at me. "Seen anyone around here?" he asked.

"No."

"Ever seen this box before?"

"Never."

He chewed at his underlip. "Could be the girl, whoever she was, had something hidden in this box and had just dug it up when she was killed."

"But I found her out on the beach."

43

"She could have been carried out there after she was dead."

"But wouldn't she have screamed or something?"

He shrugged. "Maybe whoever killed her put a hand over her mouth from behind, so she didn't get a chance to scream." He pulled a handkerchief out of his trouser pocket and wrapped it around the box. "Well, I'll take this along and have it checked for fingerprints." He started walking toward the police car, and Sergeant Kelly and I walked along with him. As he got into the car, he said, "Doesn't seem to be anything else."

I asked, "Could the body have been thrown into the water while I was down getting you?"

"If it was, it will turn up somewhere along the shore. And by the way, when you go in swimming, keep away from the rocks. They're treacherous, and there is a strong undertow all around them."

"So David Carter told me."

He looked down at me for a moment. "Why don't you go and stay at the inn? It's kind of lonely out here for a girl by herself."

I felt myself stiffen. "Because I don't want to stay at the inn. I came way out here for privacy and peace and quiet."

He shrugged. "Okay." He and Sergeant

44

Kelly got into the car. "If you need us, let us know."

I smiled. "I will. And thank you."

Out of the window of the car, he said, "I'll be seeing you."

I stood and watched him turn the car around and whizz off. I didn't like his tone of voice when he'd made that last remark. What had he meant by it? Did he think I'd killed the girl, disposed of her body, then gone in to the police with a trumped up story?

I wondered if I should drive over to David's and tell him what had happened. But how did I know he wasn't the murderer? Or the body snatcher? And what had been in the little metal box that had caused the girl to get killed?

Chapter Five

That afternoon Mrs. Whitmore drove out to see me. She had a Land-Rover. She'd changed her clothes since the morning. Now she was wearing khaki trousers and a dark blue sweater. Her head was bare, but she had on the gold hoop earrings. And she always wore the large diamond ring. I presumed it

45

was her engagement ring, although I noticed she never wore a wedding ring.

I was in the living room working on David's portrait when she arrived. She saw me and came in without bothering to knock. Without preamble she asked, "Why did you send the police to see me?"

I put down my brush and was glad the easel was turned so she couldn't see the painting. I came out from behind the easel. "I didn't."

"I saw you bring the police out here this morning. When they came back they stopped at my place." She gave me a piercing look full of accusation. "They questioned me about Coral."

I felt a chill slide up my back.

She kept looking at me. "Why did they do that?"

I decided to take a calculated risk. "Won't you sit down?" I asked, motioning to one of the chairs which was behind my painting.

Reluctantly she sat down but kept to the edge of the seat. I was too nervous to sit down. I stood before her. "What I have to say will shock you," I warned her.

"I don't shock easily." I noticed her lips were thin and bloodless-looking. She didn't have on any lipstick. She radiated animosity as she glared up at me.

46

Drawing in a deep breath, I plunged. "This morning, when I got up, there was a dead girl out on the beach. She had a knife in her back."

"So?"

"I don't want to be brutal, Mrs. Whitmore, but the girl was your granddaughter."

She jumped to her feet. Her eyes were angry. "That's ridiculous!" she cried. "I told you, Coral is down in Boston."

"Yes, you did tell me that. You also told me you had talked to her on the phone this morning."

"That's right."

She began walking to the door. I followed her. I said, "That is not true, because this morning your granddaughter was lying out here on the beach – dead!" I didn't mention finding the metal box.

She turned to face me. "Are you calling me a liar?"

"I'm telling you what I saw with my own eyes."

"Is that why you brought the police out here?"

"Yes. Only when we got here, someone had removed the body."

She began to smile. "You have a very vivid imagination," she said. "Perhaps the solitude out here is affecting you?"

47

I met her eyes. "Solitude does not affect me. *Murder* does."

"Oh, don't be silly! Nobody ever gets murdered up here." She went out the door, then turned back. "You are an artist?"

"Yes."

"That's very interesting. I've been wanting to have pictures painted of some of my birds. Would you be interested?"

"No."

She seemed surprised. "I would pay you whatever you asked."

"I am on my vacation."

"But you are painting."

"For pleasure."

"You would enjoy painting my birds. They are very beautiful."

"Yes, they are. But I am not interested in painting them."

She pushed by me, re-entered the living room and walked over to the easel. When she saw that I had been painting a portrait of David, she raised her eyebrows in surprise. "Oh! I thought you didn't know David." It was a statement, not a question.

"I don't. I've seen him only a few times."

"But this is a very good likeness of him."

"I'm doing it from memory. It's a knack I

48

have."

She looked at me speculatively. "How many times do you have to see a person to be able to paint him?"

"Once, if I put my mind to it."

"How many times did you see my granddaughter?"

"Twice. Once alive and once dead." Something warned me not to tell her about seeing Coral and David lunching at the inn.

She walked away from the easel. "Let's settle for the once alive."

"If you wish."

"Could you do a portrait of her from memory?"

"Yes. Once each way."

"What do you mean by that?"

"I could do one of her as she looked when she was alive, and one of her as she looked this morning lying on the beach – dead!"

She whirled on me. "Oh," she cried, "you're impossible!" She stalked out of the house, letting the screen door bang behind her, got into her Land-Rover and drove away. But she didn't turn around to go toward the village; she drove over to the rocks.

I stood and watched until the Land-Rover had disappeared. There must be a road that led either through the rocks or around the back of them. I would have to investigate sometime.

After Mrs. Whitmore had disappeared into the craggy rocks, I had a strong cup of tea and a sandwich. Then I stretched a fresh canvas and went to work on a portrait of Coral. First I did one of her as I remembered her when she had told me, in no uncertain terms, to stick to my painting. As I remembered her face, the eyes were a bright sky blue, the nose sort of flat and rather broad at the tip, the lips somewhat thick and drooping at the corners. Her black hair, cut short, had a natural wave.

As I worked I found myself giving the girl a somewhat vicious expression. I hadn't noticed her looking like that as she'd stood there in the bright noontime sunlight, defying me. Nor had I remembered her looking like that when she was arguing with David over the lunch table. But as I worked and the expression began to settle on the face, seemingly without my volition, I realized she really had looked like that.

I didn't do a complete, finished painting. I was able to get a likeness of her quickly, and I let it go at that.

The dead face I remembered better. It had shocked me so, it was etched on my memory deeper than I liked to have it.

I stretched another canvas, cleaned my palette and squeezed out and mixed fresh colors. For this sketch I would need grayed colors. The combination of the dark, stormy day and the greenish grayness of the dead face would need an extremely low gradation of color.

For this sketch the hair would be wet and therefore even darker than the hair on the live girl. It was also straightened out and lay dank on her skull. The eyes were closed. The nose was the same, but smudged by wet sand. The lips, also smudged with sand, seemed thinner and more relaxed than the day before in the bright sunshine.

I worked in a frenzy, wanting to get through and erase the memory of the dead face from my mind. After about an hour, I threw down my brush and stepped back to view my work. I was shocked to discover that there was no viciousness in the painting of the dead face, although the two faces – alive and dead – were unquestionably the same girl.

I cleaned my palette again, washed my brushes and turned the two paintings to the wall. I didn't want to have to look at them.

I sank down in one of the wicker chairs and tried to read, but nothing registered. It was all just words that didn't make any sense, strung together. I found myself wishing David would come. I refused to entertain the thought that maybe he had killed the girl, or taken away her dead body while I had been in the village. It could have been the man who had left the threatening note on my table. He had a face that one would associate with things like that – more the kind who would kill a girl for whatever there had been in the metal box.

I jumped up, rummaged among my art materials for a sketch pad and some charcoal and made a quick sketch of the man's face as it had looked as it passed me in the blue coupé. Charcoal was the perfect medium for getting a likeness of that face. Color would have been all wrong for him. He was definitely a black and white subject.

When I finished the sketch, I closed my pad and leaned it against the wall beside the pictures of Coral and the one of David, which I'd decided not to work on any more.

I was nervous and fidgety. I wanted to get out of the shack. But I didn't want to go to the village. Without realizing I had any definite plan, I took my purse, went out and got into my car and started to drive along slowly. I was going toward the rocks where Mrs. Whitmore had gone. They were about half a mile away. I hadn't realized they were that far.

As I drew near them I could see the road began to climb up, and back. Finally it became so steep I had to shift into second gear. There didn't seem to be anything in sight back from the rocks. As a matter of fact, the ground was rocky quite far back – rocky and sandy. Farther on, I could see the beginning of a pine forest. There didn't seem to be any signs of life. But when I finally reached the top I was high enough to see the ocean again. I stopped the car, got out and walked to the edge of what was a cliff with a deep drop down onto jagged rocks and spuming, foamy water. I shuddered and stepped back. There was no protective railing and no footpath. The rocks curved around toward the land, making a semicircular promontory. I followed it around, carefully avoiding the edge. At last I was able to see where the road led down to level ground and another beach, like my own. But on this beach there were at least a dozen shacks; fishermen's shacks. A few of them had men sitting in front of them mending nets, and way out I could see what must have been lobster fishermen tending their pots. There was no sign of either Mrs. Whitmore or her Land-Rover.

I entertained the idea of going down and talking to the fishermen who were mending their nets, then decided against it. If they didn't know of my existence, perhaps it would be just as well not to call attention to myself.

But one of the men had glanced up and

seen me. He waved and called, "Halloa there! Come on down." But I shook my head, and he got up and went into one of the shacks. I couldn't get too good a look at him, but he appeared to be of medium height, thickset, with light hair and a droopy light-colored mustache. I would have said he was in his early forties.

In a moment he came out of the shack. He had a small Polaroid type camera. He put it to his eye, deliberately aimed it at me and snapped a picture. This made me angry. The nerve of him! I turned and hurried back to my car, the strong wind from the sea pushing me along. I got into my car, turned it around and returned to my shack.

As soon as I was near enough to see, I discovered there was a police car parked beside David's station wagon. Waiting for me in the shack were Lieutenant Cory, Sergeant Kelly and David. They had turned my paintings and the drawing of the mysterious man around so they stood like an exhibit against the wall, and the three men were standing in front of them, examining them carefully.

My first reaction was annoyance, and I stopped at the door. The three men turned their heads, and their eyes met mine, which I knew must be flashing with anger. I said,

"Good afternoon, gentlemen. What can I do for you?" As I spoke, I opened the screen door and entered the room.

Lieutenant Cory spoke first. "Please forgive us for coming in when you weren't here, but we'd like to ask you a few questions. And as we didn't pass you coming out from the village, we figured you'd be returning soon."

"How so?" I walked closer to them.

Lieutenant Cory shrugged and smiled a little. "Because there isn't very far you could go in the opposite direction."

"Isn't there?"

He shook his head. "There's nothing on the other side of the rocks but a few fishing shacks."

"Perhaps I like fishing."

"Perhaps you do. If so, you could fish on this side of the rocks."

"Do you know any of the fishermen who use the shacks over there on the other side of the rocks?"

"Some of them. They come and they go."

"Do they ever come over here?"

"I've never known them to."

At that point David entered the conversation, if you could call it a conversation. He said, "Look, Jill, this isn't getting us anywhere. What has happened out here?"

"Haven't you heard?"

His jaw tightened. "Yes, of course I've heard, but it sounds crazy. I talked to Coral on the phone myself this morning."

"At what time?"

"Around ten."

"You're sure it was Coral?"

"Of course I'm sure."

"Did you call her, or did she call you?"

"She called me."

"And where was she calling from?"

"Boston. Some friends of her father live there. She's visiting them."

I went over and sank down on one of the wicker chairs and put my purse on the floor beside me. "Then who was the dead girl here on the beach when I got up this morning?"

"That's what we'd all like to find out. Not only *who* she was, but where her body is now."

I gave him a direct look. "And you don't know?"

Anger came into his eyes. "Of course I don't know! What kind of question is that?"

For a couple of seconds we glared at each other; then Lieutenant Cory asked, "Miss Grayson, do you mind telling me why you drove over to the rocks?"

I pulled my gaze away from David's. "Why should I mind?"

"Then will you tell us?"

"There is no reason I shouldn't. I drove over because Mrs. Whitmore went that way after she left here."

"Mrs. Whitmore was here?" David and Lieutenant Cory spoke in unison.

"Yes. She came about two o'clock."

"Did she have any specific reason?" Lieutenant Cory asked.

"Presumably she wanted to ask me why I'd sent the police to see her."

"But you didn't," Lieutenant Cory said. "We stopped there on our way back from here. We wanted to ask her a few questions."

"About Coral?"

"Yes."

"And she told you Coral was down in Boston?"

"She did."

"And do you believe her?"

"I might be able to doubt her, but I don't doubt David Carter."

I let that go and said, "I see you have been looking at my sketches."

Lieutenant Cory said, "Yes. I hope you don't mind."

"Not at all. I love having three strange men come into my house when I'm not here and snoop around."

"Oh, cut it out, Jill!" David said. Then,

"When did you do those sketches of Coral?"

"This afternoon after Mrs. Whitmore left."

"You mean you did them from memory?" This from Sergeant Kelly.

"Yes. They were all done from memory." I motioned to the four sketches lined up against the wall.

"And who is *that* man?" Lieutenant Cory pointed to the man who had passed me in the blue coupé.

"I don't know."

"Then where did you see him?"

I glanced at David, but his face told me nothing. I said, "He passed me in a car one day."

"Where?"

"On the road between here and the village. I was returning from shopping and a movie."

"Where was he coming from?"

"I don't know. He could have been here. Or he could have come from the other side of the rocks."

A frown appeared on Lieutenant Cory's brow. "I told you there is nothing on the other side of the rocks but a few fishermen's shacks."

"Then where did Mrs. Whitmore go? She went in that direction, and so far she hasn't come back."

Lieutenant Cory and Sergeant Kelly looked

at one another. Then Lieutenant Cory said, "Come on," and the two of them strode from the shack, got into the police car and zoomed off, leaving me alone with David Carter.

After a moment David walked over to the other wicker chair and sat down, took a battered pack of cigarettes and a folder of matches from the breast pocket of his shirt, lit a cigarette and leaned back, crossing his long legs to make himself comfortable. "What do you know about Mrs. Whitmore?"

He gave an almost imperceptible start, and seemed to be considering how he would answer my question. But I didn't want a carefully thought out answer. So I asked another question. "Would she kill her granddaughter and then hide her body?"

Surprisingly, he smiled slightly at that. "You don't mince words, do you?" he said.

"Would she?" I persisted.

He shrugged. "I doubt it. She's a hard, cold woman, and she didn't – I mean hasn't any love for her step-granddaughter, but I don't believe she'd go so far as to murder her."

I thought about that for a moment. Then I asked, "Did Coral have a mother and father alive?"

He got up, went to the screen door facing the beach and tossed his cigarette butt far out toward the again incoming tide. When he came back he sat on the edge of his chair, elbows on knees, clasped hands tight between his knees. "Nobody here knows much about Mrs. Whitmore's life after she married the man named Warren Whitmore in her late forties and went with him to New Guinea and environs. That was seven years ago. The man was about ten years older than she, and not having been a popular girl in town, she fell for his attentions."

"He wasn't a native of the neighborhood?"

"No. As a matter of fact, he was only in the village about a week, staying at the inn while his car was being repaired after an accident on the road down from Canada."

I began to get the picture. "And she had money?"

"She was the richest woman in town. Her father, Cy Phipps, had owned most of the town, and when he died he left everything to her."

"And this Warren Whitmore needed to have an expedition to the South Seas financed?"

He gave me a surprised look. "Who told you that?"

"No one. I read a lot and sometimes watched TV."

He smiled with the right side of his mouth.

60

"And it's an old story."

"Isn't it?"

He looked down at his big hands. "I suppose so."

"And when she got out to New Guinea she found he had been married before – to an Australian girl, had had a son who in turn had married a native girl and who had a daughter, Coral," he explained to me.

"And they were all waiting for the new bride – with enough money to finance their newest expedition," I finished for him.

His smile broadened. "How come you're not a writer instead of an artist?"

"You don't have to be a writer to see through a story like that."

"Perhaps you're clairvoyant or have ESP?"

"Neither. But anyone could imagine what came next: both the son, the son's wife and the granddaughter resented Warren's new wife, rich though she was."

He nodded. "I guess Isaac and his wife and daughter gave Warren's new wife a hard time, and when Warren died, or was killed, last year they ganged up on her. So she came home."

"But why did she bring Coral with her?"

"I guess Coral insisted on coming. She wanted to have a fling in America." He leaned back in his chair and crossed his legs, letting

61

his hands and forearms rest on the chair arms.

I said, "But all that doesn't tell me where *you* come into the picture."

He shifted in his chair. "I don't. I'm just a casual observer. I have troubles enough of my own."

"Was Coral – well, interested in you?"

Almost angrily he said, "Coral is interested in anything in pants."

"Which included you?"

"Yes! But believe me, it is entirely one-sided. What she wants is to marry a United States citizen so she won't have to go back to New Guinea when her passport runs out. She just has a visitor's visa."

I had to smile at his vehemence. "Oh, don't get excited. It's nothing to me one way or the other."

His eyes met mine. "Isn't it?" he asked.

My cheeks began to feel warm. "Of course not."

He got to his feet, said, "Well, this isn't getting us anywhere, and I have to get home. I guess Corey and Kelly aren't coming back this way." He walked to the back door, said, "See you," and walked out. I didn't even turn around to watch him go, because suddenly I realized my eyes were filling with tears.

Chapter Six

It was during a sleepless night that I decided to accept Mrs. Whitmore's offer to paint pictures of her birds. In that way, I figured, I would be in a position to learn more about the mysterious woman. I could arrange to be in or just outside the aviary for several hours a day, and thereby be in a position to observe without being too much in evidence.

Before driving in to offer my services the following morning, I had the urge to have a swim before breakfast. It was going to be a hot day, and the cooling of my blood would stand me in good stead and at least get me through until noontime.

Changing from my mini nightdress to a flowered bikini, I ran out of the shack and plunged into the surf. It was delicious; cold, tangy, invigorating.

I remembered the warnings I had been given to stay away from the rocks and I carefully did so, swimming just beyond the breakers and parallel with the shore, in the direction of the sand dunes and David's house. However, I knew I couldn't swim as far as his house, so I didn't even try.

Almost reaching a point opposite the sand dunes, I turned and started back, rolling over on my back and floating for a while to rest a bit. The early morning sun warmed my face, and the buoyancy of the salt water cradled my body. I felt as if I were alone in infinity. It was glorious.

Then, without warning, something grabbed my feet and I was dragged beneath the water. I struggled and kicked, trying to see what had hold of me. Could it be an inhabitant of the sea, such as an octopus? But no, I'd never heard of such a thing so close to the shore in these northern waters. And I would have sworn whatever was holding my feet and ankles were human hands. I was being pulled along beneath the water at about a swimming speed. Instinctively I knew enough to hold my breath, but I couldn't hold it forever. With one final desperate kick I was able to free myself and rise to the surface, where I gasped in the blessed air my lungs so badly needed.

When I'd managed to get my breathing back to normal, I trod water and looked around me. I had been towed much farther out than the distance from shore I'd been swimming, and I was much closer to the rocks. I could feel an undertow fighting me as I began to swim, with what little strength

I had left, back to where I would be closer to my shack. Without realizing it, I was screaming, "David! Help me!"

I had to get in to shore before the thing grabbed me again. The undertow was beginning to pull me down, and my arms and legs were getting as heavy as lead. I could hardly move them any more. I tried not to panic, but I was going beneath the dark greenish water. . . .

Something heavy was pushing down on my back. My face was on the warm sand, and water was running out of my nose and mouth. I gulped in some air and choked. The weight on my back was lifted, and I managed to roll over on my right side.

A man's voice asked, "Are you all right?" It sounded like David's voice. But it couldn't be. I was in the sea, and something was dragging me down. No, something was lifting me up. And I wasn't in the sea. I was on the beach, and the sea was in front of me. I looked around. And David was on the sand beside me. I was in his arms, and my cold, shivering body was resting against his.

Foolishly I began to cry and put my face against David's bare, wet chest. He just held me, saying, "There, there. You're all right. You're safe."

I stopped crying and looked up at his face, and he kissed my cold lips gently, tenderly.

"What happened?" I asked.

Still holding me, he said, "I came over early with your pail of water, and you weren't in the shack, so I looked around and saw you out there. You seemed to be having trouble, so I went out and got you."

I noticed now that all he had on was a pair of underpants, which were wet and clinging to him. A short distance away lay his blue jeans, shirt and sandals.

"Oh, David!" I cried, and threw my arms around his cold, wet, hard torso.

His arms around me were beginning to feel warm, and I didn't want to leave them. But after a while he said, "Come on; I'll carry you into the shack and make you some hot coffee."

I sighed and let him help me to my feet; then he picked me up and carried me into the shack, where he deposited me on my still unmade bed. Then he brought me a towel from a pile I had on a table. He said, "Get yourself dried off and into some clothes."

I looked down at myself, discovered that the two pieces of my bikini were embarrassingly askew and quickly pulled at the sheet to cover me. Then my eyes met David's. I saw his were twinkling and he was grinning at me. "Don't worry," he said. "I've been too busy saving your life to enjoy the sights." And before I could answer, he turned and left the room and went into the kitchen.

I took my time dressing, and by the time I reached the kitchen, properly clothed in my blue denim dress and espadrilles, he was also dressed, and there were two steaming cups of hot coffee on the kitchen table, and his wet underpants were hanging over the railing of the back porch in the sun.

As we sipped our coffee, he just kept looking at me until I began to feel embarrassed. Finally I said, "Okay, say it! You told me to stay away from the rocks."

He kept looking at me. "All I can say is – thank God I came along in time to get you out."

I reached a hand over to one of his that was lying on the table, and he took my cold fingers in his warm grasp. "I didn't go there deliberately," I told him. "I was floating parallel to the shore, just out beyond the breakers and nowhere near the rocks – as a matter of fact, I was down even with the sand dunes – when something grabbed my feet and ankles."

His eyes opened wide. "What was it?" he asked.

"I don't know. I was afraid it was an

octopus."

"No such things up around here. Maybe it was some seaweed."

"No. It didn't feel like something from the sea. It felt like hands, strong hands."

"Hands?" He pushed aside his coffee cup and took my hand in both of his.

"Yes. And – well, I fought and kicked. I could feel myself being towed along beneath the water, and I knew I couldn't hold my breath for very long, so I gave one last desperate kick and freed myself. And my feet seemed to kick something that felt like flesh."

His hands tightened on mine. "You couldn't see what it was?"

"No. I guess I was too scared."

He looked at me thoughtfully for a moment. "Have you ever done any scuba diving?" he asked.

I shook my head.

"Have you seen anyone scuba diving while you've been here?"

"No."

"Seen anyone out in a boat? Perhaps a fisherman?"

"Far out. Not anywhere near shore on this side of the rocks."

He looked down at my fingers and toyed with them. Then he looked up at my face again. "And when you surfaced you were over near the rocks?"

I nodded. "Yes. But why –"

He let go of my hand got up and fixed us more coffee. "I don't know. But if someone wanted to get rid of you, that would be a good way to do it."

I watched him pour the boiling water on the powdered instant coffee. "Get rid of the dame?" I asked.

He set the cup down in front of me. "That has nothing to do with what happened to you this morning."

"Could it be connected with what happened to Coral Whitmore yesterday?"

He sat down opposite me with his fresh coffee and began putting the cream substitute I had brought up with me into his cup. "That's what I'm afraid of," he said.

"And you wish I'd go home?" I looked down into my coffee, stirring it slowly.

He said, "Yes."

I did some quick thinking. I wondered if Lieutenant Cory had told him about finding the metal box. Something made me keep still about it. Finally I looked up at his tense, tight face. "I've just decided to accept Mrs. Whitmore's offer to paint some of her birds," I told him.

"Paint some of her birds? What do you mean?"

69

I explained, ending with, "Perhaps she'd let me stay at her house while I'm working."

"I doubt it. She doesn't encourage friendship."

"I don't want to get friendly with her. I just want to snoop around a bit."

He sighed and began to drink his coffee. Putting the half emptied cup down, he said, "At least it would get you away from here."

I finished my coffee and stood up on legs that I discovered were kind of shaky. "Then what are we waiting for?" I asked him.

When I arrived, Mrs. Whitemore was out back, fussing with her pets. I parked my car in the driveway and walked back. I thought she looked surprised when she saw me, but she quickly covered up. I spoke first. "Hi, Mrs. Whitmore," I said.

She turned away from the aviary. "Oh, it's you." The greeting wasn't exactly filled with warmth.

I said, "I waited for you to come back from the rocks yesterday afternoon."

"Oh? Did you want something?"

"Well, yes. After I thought about it, I decided it might be fun to paint some of your birds."

She glanced at me, and her dark eyes had a look of suspicion in them. Or was

70

it calculation? She said, "I've changed my mind about that. I think I'll just take colored photographs."

"Oh, but they wouldn't be nearly as artistic as paintings."

Her lips tightened. "They will answer my purpose just as well."

I felt let down. I hadn't expected that kind of a reception. But there was nothing I could do about it but accept her decision gracefully and withdraw. I said, "Well, I'm sorry. I'd really like to paint your birds. I think it would be fun."

She began walking toward the driveway where my car stood, and I had no choice but to follow her. "If you should change your mind," I said, "I'll be here until the end of the month."

Without turning to look at me, she said, "If you should want to leave earlier, I'll be glad to refund your money for the remaining time."

We'd reached my car by then, and she stopped and stood waiting for me. Joining her, I said, "Why did you rent the place if you didn't want anyone there?"

Her eyes met mine defiantly. "That is *my* business," she said.

I decided if it was going to be war between us, I would make a small offensive of my own. I asked, "When do you expect your

71

granddaughter back?"

Did I imagine it, or did her face pale beneath the dark weathering of her skin? "I don't know," she said, her words sharp and quick. "She may not return here. She may go back to her home in New Guinea from Boston. Her visitor's visa runs out this month."

"Then she is still in Boston?"

"Of course. And now good day. I have things to do." She turned and walked briskly to the house. I heard the screen door bang behind her.

Chapter Seven

I'd been asleep a couple of hours, having gone to bed around ten, when gradually I began to awaken. At first I didn't know what had disturbed me; then I began to realize I was smelling smoke, and it was affecting my breathing.

I sat up and looked around the room. Nothing was burning. I got up and slid my feet into my slippers and made a tour of inspection. There was nothing on fire in the shack, but out on the beach there was a fire that was causing the smoke, and as it happened, the wind was blowing in from the sea and wafting the smoke toward the shack. The only window that was open was the one in the bedroom, and the smoke was coming in that way. I ran back to the bedroom and closed and locked the window. Then I returned to the living room for a closer inspection of the fire.

The night was very dark, and I might have imagined a figure with a hideous face peering up at me from the bottom of the porch steps, but I didn't think so. There was surely someone there. Also, there was movement around the fire. Dark figures were dancing slowly, rhythmically. I wondered who they were, and why they were on my beach at that time of night. I glanced at my wrist watch, which I'd worn to bed and which had a radium dial. It was two-thirty.

Then I heard drums, beating, beating softly but persistently. Where was the sound coming from? I listened. It wasn't close enough to be coming from the figures dancing around the fire. Was it coming from the rocks somewhere?

This is ridiculous! I thought. What is going on here?

I went back to the bedroom and put on my light blue terry cloth robe, and as I was

73

slipping my arms into it a horrible mask-like face appeared at the window. It was definitely a mask, a grotesque mask, with overly large eyes and a grinning mouth showing uneven, tusk-like teeth. It was like something on a totem pole. There was just enough reflection from the fire on the beach to light up the horrible face and cast alternate red and black wavering spots on it.

I shuddered and stifled a scream. Running over to the window, I tried to get a closer look at it, but it suddenly disappeared, and I could see nothing but the darkness outside. I pulled down the shade to shut it out. Then I went back into the living room, and I did scream. There was a grotesque masked face peering in at every window, and the drums were beating louder. Or were they coming closer?

I stood in the middle of the room, too terrified to move. What should I do?

With a show of bravado which was completely absent from my trembling body, I walked to the door which opened out on the beach side of the shack. As I turned the key in the lock, the faces at the windows on that side disappeared, and I heard a scurrying of feet as the creatures got out of my way. Well, that was something. It meant they weren't brave enough to confront me. Or they didn't want me to discover who they were. My hands were shaking so I could hardly turn the knob to open the door, and how my shaking legs got out onto the small porch I'll never be able to explain.

Which direction should I go first? Should I run around the house and try to catch the other masked figures? Or should I go down to the smoky fire and find out who the dancing figures were?

My hesitation lasted only a moment, but even as I stood there someone had seen me. I should have realized the light from the fire would illuminate me and make me a perfect target. Two things whizzed past my head, one on the left side and one on the right, and with a zing hit the wall of the shack on either side of the open door.

Cautiously I turned my head and saw the arrows imbedded in the wood. Either or both could have killed me if whoever had shot them had wanted to kill me. I realized that whoever had shot them – and there must have been two people, because the arrows had whizzed through the air simultaneously – were excellent shots.

Too scared now even to simulate bravery, I turned to go back into the house. But before I could get through the doorway, something hit me on the back of the head – and that was that! I went into a blackness so deep there was no way of getting out.

The next thing I knew, or rather the next thing I realized, I was shivering, but this time with cold. My head ached unbearably, and I could hear the swish of the incoming tide. I tried to move and discovered I couldn't. I opened my eyes, and above me was the gray sky.

I looked around, and over to my left was the shack – with an arrow sticking in the wall on either side of the door into the living room. Then I hadn't dreamed the whole thing.

Suddenly it all came back to me – the grotesque masks, the smoky fire, the beating drums. But that was all gone. Now there was just me, and I was lying on the beach in my nightdress, light blue terry cloth robe and slippers. No, my slippers were gone. Anyway, I was pinned down to the beach by arrows which held my robe to the beach on both sides so I couldn't move. I tried to sit up, but I couldn't. I tried to turn over, but I couldn't.

A wave swished in and lapped at my right side. The quick memory of Coral's dead body lying almost in the same spot, with the knife in her back and the tide coming in, brought such terror to my heart that even if I'd been free to move, I wouldn't have been able to.

From the spot I was in, I couldn't see any remains of the smoky fire. Was it behind my head where I couldn't see it? Or was I lying on the spot? For in spite of the fact that I was shivering from the damp early morning breeze, my back felt warm. Not burned, but warm.

Had the creatures who had pinned me down on the sand with their arrows thought me to be dead? If not, had they counted on the tide coming in and covering me before I regained consciousness after the vicious blow on the back of my head? Would they come back, now it was day, and finish me off? Were they hiding, perhaps in the shack or out in front of it, waiting for me to show movement?

I yanked my arms, trying to free myself, but I didn't have strength enough to tear myself free. My robe was a good quality of material, and it held fast; the arrows were imbedded deeply into the sand.

At last I had to give up. I was exhausted with my futile struggles. I could feel the water now, slowly creeping beneath me as each wave came in farther than the one before it. The sand beneath me was no longer warm. Now it was wet and cold.

I closed my eyes and lay still. Was this going to be the end of my life? I'd scarcely begun it. I hadn't come anywhere near accomplishing what I'd hoped I would in my career. And I hadn't yet fulfilled myself as a woman. I'd always dreamed of marriage, children, a home, with my husband coming home to me at night. True, I'd never been able to fit Ed Harding into that particular picture, or any other man I'd ever known – until David. And now I'd never see David again. And he would never see me again – alive. The next time he saw me I would be cold and dead, like Coral. But how did I know he hadn't been one of the men behind a grotesque mask last night, or one of the dark forms dancing around the smoky fire? Only somehow I couldn't imagine David dancing around a fire – not the way those dark forms had been dancing last night.

Gradually I realized I was hearing the sound of a truck coming along the road from the village. I opened my eyes and strained my ears. Yes, it was definitely a truck, and it was coming closer. Who could it be? Mrs. Whitmore's Land-Rover didn't sound like that. And as far as I knew, David didn't have a truck. And surely the police wouldn't be driving a truck. And whoever the strange people were who were here last night, in the dark of the moon, they wouldn't have come from the sleepy little village of Pine Grove Harbor. Somehow I would have said they had come from the other side of the rocks.

The truck was stopping on the road in front of the shack. In a moment there was a pounding on the front door. Whoever it was, he mustn't get away without finding me. Even if he was one of the horrible people who had been here last night, I wanted to see him.

I began to scream – at first not loud enough; the knocking on the front door had stopped. "Oh, don't go away!" I yelled. Then I screamed louder and louder – so loud I frightened a sandpiper who had been trotting along near my bare feet.

Then a man called, "Hey! What's the matter? Where are you?" And around the corner of the shack came a middle-aged man, wearing dungarees and a T-shirt. He wasn't very tall, but had broad shoulders and powerful-looking arms. From one hand dangled large tongs with sharp points. I screamed loud enough to split the gray heavens wide open. And maybe I did, because suddenly it began to rain.

The man dropped the tongs and ran over to me. Then he stood and stared. "Fer gosh sake!" he said. "What happened to *you?*"

I had stopped screaming and just looked up at him. His black hair was graying at the temples, and he had enormous brown eyes. Then my teeth began to chatter so I couldn't speak. But I didn't have to. Without

79

asking any more questions, the man leaned over and began to pull up the arrows. When he'd tossed aside the last one, he helped me to get up. But I couldn't stand, so he picked me up and carried me into the house and put me in one of the wicker chairs in the living room. Then he stood in front of me and put his hands on his hips. "I wouldn't have believe it if I hadn't seen it!" he observed.

Gasping, I managed to ask, "Who are you?"

"The iceman. Do you want any ice today?"

Unexpectedly I began to laugh; then I began to cry; then I laughed again.

The man stood watching me for a few minutes; then he slapped me in the face, once on each cheek. "Shut up!" he said.

For a few moments I sobbed silently; then I was able to stop. The man said, "I'm sorry but I had to do that. You were hysterical."

I nodded.

"Want me to go get the police?" he asked.

I shook my head.

"Want to come into town with me?"

I shook my head again.

"But you can't stay here alone after what's happened to you. Who did it?"

"I don't know."

"Didn't you see?"

I shook my head.

"Well, you can't just stay here!"

I shivered. I was still cold, right to the very core.

"Got any friends around here?"

I shook my head.

"Not even old lady Whitmore?"

I shrugged.

"What about that guy down the beach?"

I shrugged again.

"Well, I don't like to go and leave you here alone. What do you want me to do?"

My head was aching and I put a hand up to where it hurt most. I felt a large lump there. I wondered what I'd been hit with. It would have taken more than an arrow to make a lump like that. I said, "Somebody hit me on the head. It hurts." I looked at my watch. It was a little after seven. As I did so, the man took a large watch from a small front pocket in his dungarees. "I make this my first stop," he explained. "Good thing I did."

I said, "I guess I'd better have some ice."

It was then I noticed my paintings were gone. Not the one of the sand dunes or the charcoal sketch of the man in the blue coupé, but the two paintings of Coral, alive and dead, and one of David. I said, "Maybe I will go back with you. Could you wait a few minutes until I get dressed?"

The man said, "Sure. Take your time."

Chapter Eight

As we were driving toward the village, the iceman, whose name was Joe, asked me, "Where do you want me to take you?" I was sitting on the seat beside him, which was narrow and high up from the road. I'd put on a pair of black chinos, a white blouse and a black cable stitch coat sweater. I hadn't brought a bag; just my purse. I would have to go back for my things later. When I didn't answer Joe's question, he asked another. "Want I should take you to a doctor?"

I said, "Maybe. My head aches, and I'm still cold."

Joe said, "I could take you to my place. My wife would take care of you."

I turned my head and smiled at him. He had a strong face with regular features which were lined, as if life hadn't been too easy for him. "Thank you," I said. "That's very kind of you. But I guess I'd better go to a doctor first, and then to the police."

He shrugged. "Okay."

The sun was beginning to come out, and the sea grass on either side of the sandy road was ruffling as the breeze swept across it. The ice truck was open in front, and as the breeze hit me I wrapped my sweater close around me. I hadn't thought to tie anything around my hair, and it kept blowing in my face. I breathed deeply of the salt air. I'd always liked the smell of the sea. I asked Joe, "Do you know anything about what is on the other side of those rocks out at Sand's End?"

He honked the horn at a small animal that scuttled from the sea grass and across the road. "There isn't anything over there," Joe said, "but some fishermen's shacks."

"Who owns them?"

"I wouldn't know. I guess different people. The other side of those rocks doesn't belong to Pine Grove Harbor."

"Would it be possible for a person to rent one of those shacks?"

He glanced at me curiously. "You thinking of going over there?"

"No. I was just wondering. Are there just fishermen there or do other people besides fishermen use them?"

"I wouldn't know. Sometimes there's fights over there, but mostly it's quiet."

"Could the people who invaded my place last night have come from over there?"

"What folks?"

"Well, the folks with the arrows and the masks."

"Masks?"

"Yes." I sighed. "I guess I'd better tell you the whole story." So I did. When I finished he said, "Sounds crazy. Maine fishermen aren't vicious like that. They just fish for a living and drink a little sometimes. Then they might fight among themselves. But they wouldn't do anything like what happened to you. And they wouldn't have arrows – unless for hunting."

As we drove past the Whitmore place, we could hear the weird noises made by the birds. I asked, "Do you deliver ice to Mrs. Whitmore?"

He said, "No. She's near enough to the village to have electricity. The only folks who need any kind of ice these days are on the outskirts of town, like your shack out at Sand's End, and some of the very old houses out in the country that never got around to having electricity put in or gas piped in."

"Are there many of those?"

"Not many. The only reason I bother with them is because my father used to service them. Now I sell coal and fuel oil in the winter and do a little farming in the summer and deliver ice."

We were coming to the village, and he said,

"There's a doctor down on the main street. Old man who's brought most of the town people into the world. Name's Dr. Cabot."

"He sounds nice."

"He is. He'll take care of you all right."

When Joe stopped the truck in front of a large old-fashioned white clapboard house with a small gold-lettered sign on the railing of the wide porch proclaiming that Dr. Cabot's office hours were 10-12:6-8, I asked, "How much do I owe you, Joe?"

He raced the motor of the truck. When it quieted down, he said, "I'll bring you a bill for the ice when you're ready to leave Sand's End."

"I don't mean for the ice. I mean for being so kind as to drive me into the village."

He turned and looked at me. "Folks in Pine Grove Harbor don't charge for being friendly," he said.

I felt rebuked and knew my face was getting red. "Forgive me," I said. "I'm from the city. Down there you have to pay for everything."

He revved the motor again. "Forget it," he said, waiting for me to get out of the truck.

It wasn't easy, feeling the way I did, but I managed. When I was standing down on the road I looked up at him. "Thanks, Joe," I said. "And would you mind not telling

85

anybody about how you found me on the sand?"

He seemed surprise. "You're going to tell the police, aren't you?"

"Yes, but – well, I'd rather not have it talked about until we find out who did it. Understand?"

"You're the boss," he said. "But if I was you, I wouldn't go back out there any more."

I nodded in agreement. "I doubt if I shall. Not alone, anyway."

He started the truck, and I moved back with a wave of my hand, calling, "Thank you."

It was far too early for Dr. Cabot's morning office hours, but when I rang the bell he came to the door himself. He was tall and gaunt, with straight white hair parted on the side and brushed back, and kindly, faded blue eyes. "Good morning," he said cheerfully.

I said, "Good morning, Dr. Cabot. I'm Jill Grayson. I've been renting Mrs. Whitmore's beach shack out at Sand's End, and I've had an accident. Could I see you for a few minutes?"

He said, "Of course," and stepped aside so I could enter the hall. Then he preceded me to the back of the hall and into his office, had me sit in a chair beside his desk and then sat in an old black leather swivel chair before the desk.

86

"Now then," he said, "tell me about it."

See me hesitate, he said, "You've been hurt?"

I nodded, and that made my head hurt worse. I touched the lump carefully. "My head," I said. "Something fell on it."

"Fell on it?" He got up and walked around behind me.

I said, "Yes."

Gently he examined the back of my head. His probing fingers made me wince. After a moment he asked, "Know what hit you?"

"No." Well, that was the truth. I *didn't* know.

He went to a cabinet at the side of the room, wet a piece of cotton with some colorless liquid, then came back to me and dabbed the wet cotton on my head. It stung, and I said, "Ouch!"

"It's probably not as bad as it feels. Any nausea?"

"No."

"Feel dizzy?"

"No."

"Then it isn't a concussion. If you want, you can go over to the hospital and have it X-rayed."

"I'd rather not, if you don't think it's necessary."

"I really don't. It seems like a contusion

87

rather than a concussion. Had any breakfast?"

"No."

He took a couple of white pills from a bottle in a desk drawer, got a paper cup of water and said, "Take these. They'll quiet your nerves."

"But I'm not nervous."

"Aren't you?" He looked at my hand holding the paper cup of water. It was shaking so the water was making waves. I took the pills and swallowed some of the water, handing him the cup.

Then all of a sudden I began to cry. I covered my face with my cold, trembling hands and cried silently.

"Without saying a word, Dr. Cabot left the room. He was gone quite a while, and when I was able to stop crying, get some tissues from my purse and wipe my face, I glanced around the office. I was beginning to feel sleepy. At one side of the room there was an old-fashioned black leather couch. I got up and went over to it and lay down, turning my head to one side so I wouldn't have to lie on the lump on the back of my head.

The next thing I knew there was a middle-aged woman in a nurse's uniform standing beside me. She smiled. "How do you feel?" She had a cup of coffee in her hand.

I said, "I don't know. I guess I'm all right."

She said, "Good. Now suppose you sit up

and drink this. The doctor had to go out, but he'll be back in a few minutes. It's almost ten o'clock, and his office hours start then."

I managed to sit up with her help, and she gave me the coffee. It was hot and delicious, and I began to realize I was hungry. My head didn't hurt as badly as it had. Now there was just a dull ache.

While I was drinking the coffee, the front doorbell rang a couple of times, and the nurse went to admit the first of the office patients.

When she returned to me I'd finished the coffee. I said, "Well, I guess I'd better go." I managed to get to my feet, but I couldn't walk very well. The nurse took the cup and saucer, put them on a side cabinet and caught me just as my knees gave way. I sank down on the couch again.

The nurse said, "You'd better stay here until Dr. Cabot gets back."

I didn't reply to that. I didn't know what to say. I didn't know where to go. I couldn't return to the shack out at Sand's End, and there wasn't any place else for me to go, unless I got a room at the inn. I was in no condition to drive to New York, even if I had had my car in the village.

Dr. Cabot came in briskly, set his black bag on the desk and said, "Well, how do you feel now?"

"I seem to be –"

"She's very weak, Doctor," the nurse said. "She slept a couple of hours, and she's had a cup of coffee, but she isn't well enough to go out alone."

The doctor came over to me, picked up my hand and took my pulse. When he finished he said, "You seem to be in a state of shock. Do you want to tell me just what happened to you?"

He pulled up a chair and sat down beside me. I looked up into his kindly eyes and decided I'd better tell him to whole story. He nodded to the nurse, and she left the room.

When I'd finished, he sat thinking for a few moments. Then he said, "You're renting the shack from Mrs. Whitmore?"

"Yes."

"Perhaps you should tell her about last night."

I raised myself on one elbow. "Oh no!" I said. "I wouldn't want her to know."

"She's a very nice woman, and she has a big house. You could stay with her until you're well enough to go home."

"No, she wouldn't want me."

"Why not?"

"Well, she asked me to paint pictures of some of her birds. And then later she didn't want me to."

90

He smiled.

"It's not only that," I said. "I think something strange is going on." I sighed and lay back again. "Oh, I don't know what to do."

"Perhaps you should tell the police what happened to you last night?"

"I was going to, after I'd seen you about my head. But now I don't think I could make it to the police station."

Dr. Cabot stood up, replaced the chair he'd been sitting on and said, "Suppose we ask Lieutenant Cory to come here? You can go upstairs and lie down, and my wife will stay with you." He went to the door and called the nurse. "Miss Jennings, please ask Mrs. Cabot to come in."

The nurse nodded and went through the hall, and Dr. Cabot went to his desk and called the police station. When he got Lieutenant Cory, he explained, "I have a patient here in my office, a Miss Jill Grayson. She's been having some trouble out at Sand's End, and I think you ought to know about it. Can you come over to my place? She isn't able to get to you."

From across the room I could hear Lieutenant Cory's voice rasp, "Be right over."

Just then a short, plump, pretty woman with white hair, wearing a flowered house dress, came into the office. Dr. Cabot said, "This is my wife. Nellie, this is Jill Grayson. I wish you'd take her upstairs and let her rest in the guest room for a while. She's expecting a visitor in a few minutes: Lieutenant Cory."

Mrs. Cabot said, "Of course," and came over to help me up, but it took both her and the nurse to get me upstairs. I'd never in my life felt so helpless.

When we were in a large, cheerful corner room, with a hooked rug on the floor, a big four poster spool bed with a white hand-crocheted spread in one corner, and old-fashioned black walnut furniture, Mrs. Cabot said, "Now you lie down, and I'll sit with you until Billy comes."

"Billy?"

She smiled. "Lieutenant Cory to you. I've known him ever since he was born, so he's Billy to me."

She was leading me to the bed, but I held back. "I don't want to lie on that nice white lace spread."

She let me sit in the rocking chair, saying, "I'll get something to put over it." Then, going to the closet, she took from a shelf a handmade patchwork quilt and spread it over the bed. "There," she said. "Just take off your shoes."

I had on black denim sneakers with white

92

rubber soles and white laces. I kicked them off. While I was doing that, she pulled the two white-cased pillows from beneath the spread and placed them on top of the quilt. Then she came to me and helped me from the rocking chair over to the bed. I sank back on the softness with a grateful sigh. "Thank you. You're very kind."

She just smiled and patted my hand. Then she went and sat in the rocking chair. I closed my eyes and she said, "Better not sleep until after Billy has been here, and you've had some lunch."

I opened my eyes. "I don't know why I feel so bushed. I'm usually as strong as an ox."

"You'll be all right again soon."

I sighed. "I'd better be. I want to go home."

We heard footsteps coming up the stairs, and Mrs. Cabot jumped up, went into the hall and said brightly. "Good morning, Billy. How's the family?"

Lieutenant Cory said, "Good morning, Aunt Nellie. Everybody's fine."

She said, "In here," and in a moment she returned to the room, followed by Lieutenant Cory. When he saw me lying on the bed, he said, "So we meet again."

I said, "Yes."

He looked around the room, saw a straight-backed chair with a rush seat and brought it over to the side of the bed, hung his hat on one of the bedposts at the foot of the bed and said, "Now tell me about it."

Mrs. Cabot said, "Excuse me. I'll leave you two alone," went out and closed the door.

Lieutenant Cory and I looked at each other, and after a moment I said, "I hardly know how to tell you about what happened last night. It sounds like something from an Alfred Hitchcock movie."

"Just start at the beginning," Lieutenant Cory said, bringing his right foot up so he could rest the ankle on his left knee. So I began to talk. I began at the place where I had awakened and smelled smoke. I told him everything right up to that very minute. When I finished he looked at me thoughtfully and, I thought, doubtfully.

I said, "At least Joe, the iceman, can corroborate the part about finding me pinned down to the beach with arrows. And the two arrows are still sticking in the woodwork on either side of the door on the beach side of the shack."

He let his right foot slide off his left knee, and it thudded down on the floor. "Um," he said. "Well, we'll see. I'll take a couple of men out there."

He stood up and started for the door; then he turned. "It seems to me that old lady Whitmore should be responsible for you. I'll stop in and see her on my way."

I sat up on the bed. "Oh no! Please don't! I don't want to get mixed up with her any more than I have been."

He came back to the bed and took his hat from the post. "You know what I wish you'd do?" he said.

I shook my head.

"I'd like you to go and stay with Mrs. Whitmore for a while and see what you can find out. If she's mixed up in these strange happenings, maybe you can find out, if you're right there in the house."

I drew in a sharp breath. "But if she's involved in the happenings out at Sand's End, I wouldn't be safe there in her house."

He thought about that for a moment, put on his hat, then shoved it on the back of his head. "If you were staying there in her house and she knew we knew you were there, she wouldn't dare let anything happen to you."

"But suppose it is someone she doesn't know anything about?"

"That's what I'd like to find out."

"But I'd be terrified! It's such a big, spooky-looking old house."

He looked at me, and then suddenly he

95

grinned. "Chicken?" he asked teasingly.

I shivered, but I also got angry. Nobody had ever called me "chicken" before. "No, of course not," I said with a toss of my aching head, "except that I don't relish being murdered."

"I could have a talk with David Carter," he suggested; "ask him to make it a point of visiting the Whitmore place frequently." He gave me a big boyish grin. "He could pretend he was sweet on you – or something like that."

I glared at him. "Why don't you just take out your gun and shoot me?"

He laughed. "Oh, come now; David isn't that bad." And with a salute he opened the door and went out. Then he came back. "Besides," he said, "I'll be in and out of the house for a few days myself. Mrs. Whitmore phoned us this morning and said she'd lost some jewelry and unset precious stones."

I put my hand to my head. "Oh, great!" I said. "That's all we need!" Then I asked, "Did you find out anything about the metal box?"

He waited a moment before answering me; then he said, "It's covered with fingerprints – Coral's and Mrs. Whitmore's."

"How did you get theirs to compare with those on the box?"

"When she reported her jewelry missing, it gave me an excuse to take fingerprints around the house."

"Does Mrs. Whitmore know about the metal box?"

"Not yet. And don't tell her."

"I won't."

Chapter Nine

As soon as Lieutenant Cory had left, Mrs. Cabot came back, accompanied by a maid carrying a tray of lunch for me. The maid was young, rosy-cheeked and sturdy-looking. Mrs. Cabot said, "This is Carry, Miss Grayson. Carry has brought you some lunch, and then you can sleep for a while."

The girl smiled at me, and Mrs. Cabot fixed the pillows so I would be sitting up. Then Carry placed the tray on my lap. It had legs so the weight didn't rest on *my* legs.

Everything looked delicious. There was a bowl of steaming New England clam chowder, hot biscuits, homemade warm blueberry pie and a pot of tea.

Having settled the tray so everything was within my reach, Carry went downstairs.

But Mrs. Cabot stayed with me, ensconcing herself in the rocking chair again. "You'll feel better after you've eaten," she said.

I began to eat. "I'm sure I shall," I told her. "Everything is wonderful."

After that we didn't talk for a while, and I began to feel myself relaxing and beginning to get warm, as the hot chowder filled my empty stomach. Finally Mrs. Cabot said, "You'll be all right now Billy's taking care of you."

"Taking care of me?"

"Yes. He's as smart they come. It's like they say of the Canadian Royal Mounties. He always gets his man."

When I'd finished my lunch, Mrs. Cabot took the tray and put it on the floor just outside the bedroom door. "Carry will get it later," she said. "Now you try and sleep. Let me fix your pillows."

She did, then pulled down the shades and, throwing a light crocheted afghan over me, said, "I'll close the door so you won't hear the patients coming and going."

I smiled my gratitude. "You're very kind. Thank you."

After she'd left me I closed my eyes, not meaning to sleep, but I must have, because when I awoke it was late afternoon. My wrist watch said 4:30. I moved my head and discovered it felt better. Then the door opened and Mrs. Cabot came into the room, followed by Mrs. Whitmore. "I'm glad you're awake," she said. "Did you have a nice nap?"

I said, "Yes, I guess so."

She came to the bed and helped me to sit up, arranging the pillows to support my back.

Mrs. Whitmore came and stood beside the bed and looked down at me. She had on gray slacks, a white tailored blouse, the inevitable gold hoop earrings and the big diamond ring. "I hear you've been having trouble out at Sand's End," she said.

I said, "Yes. And if you don't mind, I don't think I want to go back there."

She raised her eyebrows. "Suit yourself. I told you I'd refund your money any time you wanted to leave."

"You don't have to do that."

"In the meantime," she said, "Lieutenant Cory seems to think I should be responsible for you."

I glanced at Mrs. Cabot, but she just smiled sweetly.

Mrs. Whitmore said, "You'd better come with me now. I haven't much time. I have things to do for the birds. Can you walk?"

I said. "I don't know. I'll try." I sat up and put my legs over the side of the bed, my feet on the floor. Then I tried to stand up. To my surprise, I found I could. Mrs. Cabot took my arm. "Would you rather stay here?" she asked me.

I certainly would rather have stayed there, but if Lieutenant Cory wanted me to go to the Whitmore place, I felt that was what I should do. So I said, "Thank you, but I've been enough bother to you."

"No bother at all," Mrs. Cabot assured me.

I managed to get down the stairs by holding onto the bannister on one side and Mrs. Cabot holding my arm on the other. Mrs. Whitmore stalked down ahead of us.

Out on the front porch, she said, "Well, Nellie, I'll call you."

Mrs. Cabot said, "Yes, do, Agnes. I'll be anxious to know how Miss Grayson is. And if she needs the doctor, be sure and call him. He'll come right out."

Mrs. Whitmore just grunted and went down the porch steps and out to the Land-Rover which stood before the house.

Mrs. Cabot went with me to the car and helped me up into it. "You sure you'll be all right?" she asked me anxiously.

I said, "Yes. And thank you."

During the drive from the doctor's to the Whitmore place, my reluctant hostess didn't speak to me. When she drove the Land-Rover into her driveway, the birds were screeching as usual.

I managed to get out of the car by myself, and she got out the other side. As we went up the front porch, she said, "You'll find it very dull here."

"I hope I shan't have to inconvenience you for long." I resented her attitude toward me as much as she resented having me there. She shoved me into the house ahead of her and called, "Mary!"

We were in a large square hall with a room on either side and broad stairs going up at the left. The bannisters were painted white, and the handrail was mahogany. The stairs were mahogany, with the risers painted white. I heard a door open, and a plump elderly woman in a housedress with a large white apron tied around her waist ambled into the hall from a room at the back which I could see was the kitchen. Mrs. Whitmore said, "She's here," jerking her head in my direction.

The woman called Mary said, "You go on and tend to the birds. I'll show her where she's to be put."

Mrs. Whitmore said, "All right," and without a word to me, went through the wide center hall to the kitchen.

Mary said, "You come with me," and began to climb the stairs. I followed, feeling like a child who had just been left at an orphanage.

101

The second floor hall was square like the downstairs, and bedrooms opened off from it on three sides; the fourth was taken up by the stairs and a railing that went from them over to a wall that must have been the wall to a bedroom.

"Over here," Mary said, and went into a room at the right. I followed her and glanced curiously around. It was a large square room, papered in a white satiny paper with big cabbage roses splashed on it. The furniture was mahogany, and the bureau had a marble top, also a commode which held a bowl and pitcher. Just as I was wondering if the house didn't have running water, Mary said, "There's a bathroom down at the other side of the hall." She went to a window and straightened a shade. There were two windows, and both were open, with screens in them.

I could hear the birds screeching, and when I went over to a window I saw I was at the back of the house and could look out over the aviary.

"Them birds drive me crazy," Mary grumbled. "Always screeching!"

"Do they screech all night?" I asked her.

"Some of them, because some of them are night birds. There's even one they call a ghost bird, no less."

102

I turned and looked at Mary. She had a round face with a weathered outdoors look. Her hair was brown, well sprinkled with gray. Her eyes were kind of green, and her teeth were too perfect to be anything but false. I asked, "Have you been here long?"

She sighed. "Since I was a girl. I worked for the Phipps, and then when they died I stayed on with Agnes."

"And when she married and went away?"

"I stayed here and took care of the house. She didn't want to sell it. She and her husband came back occasionally. Out back there used to be just fields until she came back this year with them birds."

"Don't you like the birds?"

"Some of them are all right. But I don't like queer things, like some of them. The ghost-bird, for instance."

"Oh? What does that look like?"

"Well, kind of like an enormous owl. Only instead of sitting up straight, he sits down low and flat. And he has a long tail like a swallow stretching out behind. And he has big red eyes, and he makes snapping noises with his bill that's about six inches wide, like a frog's mouth. And he makes a kind of sighing noise. Ugh!" She shuddered at the very thought of him.

I had to smile at her graphic description.

"Well, some of them are quite beautiful."

At that she just grunted and ambled over to the door. "If you want anything, I'll be down in the kitchen. There's back stairs down there near the bathroom. And your towels are the blue ones."

I said, "Thank you, Mary."

"Dinner's at six. I ring a bell. You'll hear it."

Again I said, "Thank you."

When she'd gone, I closed the door and looked more carefully at the room. The bed was a large double bed with a high, carved headboard and a footboard about half as high. It had a clean white candlewick spread. There was one upholstered chair with antimacassars, beside which was a marble-topped table. On the table was a china kerosene lamp with roses painted on the base and the china shade, but it had been wired for electricity. Also on the table was a worn and very old-looking Bible. There were two cane-seated straight-backed chairs and a large double-doored wardrobe that reached nearly to the ceiling. I went over to it and opened one of the doors. There were several dresses in it, and one of them was the colorful shift Coral had had on the day she'd come across the sand dunes to warn me to stick to my painting. I shuddered and closed the door.

I went to one of the windows. Mrs. Whitmore was in the aviary. She was doing something to the back of the bowerbird's hut. At the side of the wire fence was a tall, thin, dark-skinned man, wearing dungarees and a blue-and-white-striped T-shirt. On his head was a black velvet Mohammedan hat around which his thatch of Papuan-type hair stuck out rather wildly. He was raking along close to the fence; leaves, twigs, debris blown there by the wind. From his ears dangled gold hoop earrings, similar to those Mrs. Whitmore always wore. I wondered if he was someone she had brought back with her from New Guinea.

I found out later that he was, and his name was Saban. Mary didn't like him. As a matter of fact, I think she was afraid of him. I met him first when, at the sound of the dinner bell, I washed my hands, tried to smooth my hair without benefit of either comb or brush and went downstairs. I didn't know where the dining room was, but I could hear voices and dishes clattering from a room at the back of the hall. I went to the doorway and saw Mrs. Whitmore sitting at a large round table which was set as if for company. There was a white damask cloth, shining silver, sparkling glassware and beautiful china edged with gold. A low bowl of variegated flowers was in the center of the table, and two silver candelabra with lighted candles gave the only light in the room. It was still light outdoors, so the candles were for show rather than for utility.

Mrs. Whitmore had changed into a simple black dress with a touch of white lace at the neck. Somehow a dress did not become her. When she saw me she said, "Come over here by me," and indicated a place which was set near her.

Standing in the doorway to the kitchen was the dark-skinned man I had seen from my bedroom window. He had been talking to Mrs. Whitmore when I entered the room. Now she said, "Miss Grayson, this is Saban. He helps me with the birds."

The man nodded and smiled, I could see he had a couple of gold teeth. I said, "How do you do, Saban."

To my surprise, he said, "Hi. See you aroun'," went into the kitchen and let the door swing to behind him.

Noticing my surprise, Mrs. Whitmore said, "Saban is my right-hand man. He's Malaysian, but he's always worked for American, English and Dutch people, and he's picked up phrases from each of them and uses them at the most unexpected times."

Before I could answer, Mary came in with

106

a large platter on which there was a piece of corned beef, surrounded by small white boiled potatoes and small whole carrots. It smelled delicious. Mrs. Whitmore said, "I hope you don't mind a New England boiled dinner?"

"I love it," I hastened to assure her. "At home we used to have corned beef and cabbage once a week, but when you live alone you don't bother much with food."

Mary put the platter on the table in front of Mrs. Whitmore and returned to the kitchen. As she carved the corned beef, Mrs. Whitmore said, "I should think a pretty girl like you would be married. What about Ed Harding?"

I felt my cheeks flush. "I've been too busy earning a living," I said. "But some day I hope to marry, although I doubt if it will be Ed Harding."

Mrs. Whitmore raised her eyebrows and spooned potatoes and carrots on the plate beside the slices of corned beef, and Mary came in with a large round dish of cabbage. Mrs. Whitmore asked her, "Has Saban had his dinner?"

"He's eating now," Mary said. "I feed him first. Then I eat in peace."

Mrs. Whitmore shrugged. "Suit yourself." She gave me the plate she'd been filling. I took it, and Mary came to my side with the dish of cabbage. As I took a spoonful of it, she said, "You got a bag with your nightdress and things?"

I said, "No, I haven't, Mary. I'll just have to do without for tonight."

Mrs. Whitmore said, "Do you want Saban to drive out and get your things for you?"

I didn't know what to say to that. I wanted my things, but I didn't like the idea of Saban handling my personal possessions, such as underwear and toilet articles. Seeing my hesitation, Mrs. Whitmore said, "Mary could go out with him and pack your things. Unless you want to go yourself?"

A shiver went through me at the thought of ever returning to Sand's End, and I quickly said, "Oh no! I don't want to go. But I would like to get my clothes and art materials. My car can stay there until – well, tomorrow."

Mrs. Whitmore began to eat. She had a thoughtful look on her face. In a couple of moments she asked, "Mary, is Saban going out this evening?"

Mary shrugged. "I don't know. He doesn't tell me what he does – after hours."

Mrs. Whitmore's lips tightened; then she said, "Why don't we all go out to Sand's End as soon as we finish dinner? It will still be light, and I'd like to look the place over

108

myself." She glanced at me. "You seem to be all right now. I'm sure it wouldn't hurt you to ride out with us. Then you can oversee the packing of your things." She was watching my face as she spoke. "Surely you wouldn't be afraid to go out there with Mary and me and Saban?" She smiled a little. "Saban is a strong man and a brave fighter. He will protect us." I had the feeling she had said the last for the benefit of Saban, who was probably in the kitchen listening.

Whatever the reason, it was a challenge to me, and I couldn't very well refuse. Besides, I would like to be there when my bags were packed and do as much of it myself as my strength would permit.

When we got back to the Whitmore place, David was waiting for us, his station wagon parked on the road. He was standing on the porch, looking worried. He came to me first. "Are you all right?" he asked, gripping my shoulders in his strong hands.

We had all gotten out of the Land-Rover and were standing in the driveway. Mrs. Whitmore had parked my car directly behind the Land-Rover, which Saban had driven. It was beginning to get dark by that time, and some of the birds had stopped screeching, others had commenced. I said, "I guess I'm all right," and managed a small smile.

"Lieutenant Cory told me about it," David said. "I hope *now* you'll get away from there."

Meekly I said, "Yes. Last night did it."

David's hands dropped to his sides, and he turned to Mrs. Whitmore. "You know?" he asked.

She nodded. "Yes, I know." I thought her voice sounded suddenly weary.

"Those masks," David said.

She just nodded. Saban was the one who spoke. "Devil masks," he said.

Mrs. Whitmore said, "Keep still, Saban. Go tend to your work."

He shrugged. "Okay, Tuan," he said.

"You know what it means?" David asked Mrs. Whitmore.

She nodded. "Yes, he's here. I've seen him. He's over in one of the shacks on the other side of the rocks."

"Did you talk to him?"

"Yes."

"Did you ask him about Coral?"

"Yes. He says he hasn't seen her."

"Do you believe him?"

"Of course."

"Then where is she?"

"Oh, for heaven sakes!" Mrs. Whitmore cried. "Down in Boston. You talked to her yourself!"

David's face was tense, and his fists clenched at his sides. "Did I? Did you? We talked to a girl who sounded like Coral. But was it?"

A look of fear came across Mrs. Whitmore's face. "Of course it was," she said.

"Then call her now. You know where she was going?"

"Of course I know where she was going. To those friends of her father's."

"Do you have their number?"

"Yes, of course I have it."

"Then come into the house and call them."

For a moment Mrs. Whitmore hesitated; then, with a gesture of hopelessness, she said, "All right. Come on." She led the way into the house, and David and I followed her. Mary went on through the square front hall and into the kitchen.

There was a phone on a side table beneath the stairs. I hadn't noticed it earlier. To David and me, Mrs. Whitmore said, "Wait in the living room." She indicated the room at the right of the front door.

It was a typical, old-fashioned, turn-of-the-century type of room.

David and I sat down on a large, ugly brown plush sofa, and he took hold of my hand. We could hear Mrs. Whitmore talking on the phone. She had been connected with the person she was calling. She asked, "Is Coral Whitmore there? This is Agnes."

Then after a moment, "She isn't?"

"Has she been there?

"Do you know where she is?

"Haven't you heard from her at all?

"Not since she wrote and said she was coming?

"But then where is she?

"No, she isn't here. If she was, I wouldn't be calling you. She left for Boston. Not the night before last – the evening before that.

"No, she wasn't driving. She was taking the train. She could walk to the station from here. No, I didn't go with her.

"Well, all right. Yes, I'm well, Goodbye."

The receiver was dropped into place with a bang, and Mrs. Whitmore came and stood in the doorway. She was very white, beneath the weathered tanned skin of her face. She opened her lips to speak; then without uttering a sound she collapsed, hitting the highly polished floor with a loud thud.

Mary came running in from the kitchen, calling, "What was that?"

She reached her mistress at the same time David and I did, and the three of us went down on our knees beside the prostate woman; Mary on one side of her and David and I on the other. Then suddenly, from outside, a bird began to screech louder than the others. It sounded frightened. I looked up at David. He said, "Sounds like the bowerbird. Someone must be too close to his bower." He got to his feet. "You and Mary stay with her." He nodded to Mrs. Whitmore. "I'll go out back and see what's the matter."

Chapter Ten

Mary and I worked over Mrs. Whitmore for quite a while before we were able to bring her to. Then Mary got some brandy and held it to her lips, while I put an arm under her and held her up so she could sip the warm, comforting liquid. After a few sips she turned her head away from the glass. "No more," she murmured.

Mary put the glass on a table, and together we managed to get Mrs. Whitmore to her feet and into the living room, where we laid her down on the ugly brown plush sofa. There were several small pillows which we shoved under her head, and she heaved a great sigh and closed her eyes again.

Mary and I stood beside her for a few

minutes; then Mary said, "Agnes, what happened?"

Mrs. Whitmore opened her eyes and glared at me. "It's all *your* fault!" she told me.

"*My* fault? How?"

"If you hadn't come up here, nothing would have happened."

"That's nonsense!" I said, angry now and reaching the breaking point.

"If you hadn't been out there at Sand's End –"

"Then why did you rent me the shack?"

She sighed and closed her eyes again. "Needed the money."

Mary said, "Agnes, you know that's not true."

"You mind your own business," Mrs. Whitmore told her, keeping her eyes closed.

I asked, "What about Coral?"

Her eyes snapped open, and a look of fear came into them. "She never reached Boston," she said, as if it were an effort to get out each word.

"Then who called you on the phone?"

"I don't know. Maybe she was calling from somewhere else."

That I couldn't answer without being brutal. Fortunately, David came in just then. When he saw Mrs. Whitmore lying on the sofa, he came over to her. "You all right?" he asked.

She said, "Yes. I guess I fainted."

David asked, "What about Coral?"

I answered for her. "She never reached Boston."

He chewed at his lips and avoided meeting my eyes. I asked, "Did you discover what was the trouble out back?"

"It was nothing. Saban was clearing up around the bowerbird's bower, and the bird got excited."

Mrs. Whitmore sat up then. She looked very angry. "Saban has no right to touch the bowerbird's bower, and he knows it!" She looked up at Mary. "Go get him!" she said. "Tell him I want to see him. At once!"

Mary turned and left the room, and Mrs. Whitmore swung her feet and legs around so she was in a sitting position on the sofa, leaning back, but looking very uncomfortable. I took one of the pillows and slid it behind her head, and she said, "Thank you." Then, "When Saban comes in, I want to speak to him alone. You two go – oh, I don't care where you go. Just get out. Leave me alone." She raised her voice on the last sentence so it was nearly a scream.

David put an arm around my shoulders. "Come on," he said; "we'll take a drive." I

115

nodded and let him lead me out of the house and help me into his station wagon, which was parked out on the road.

We drove through the village, past the inn, which was brightly lighted past the movie house, the various stores, the police station, Dr. Cabot's house, and on out a country road, up over a hill. Then, stopping on a walled promontory where several other cars were parked, he turned off the motor and lights and said, "Now then, tell me exactly what's been happening to you."

He lit a couple of cigarettes and gave me one.

"You said Lieutenant Cory told you."

"He did. But I want to hear it from you."

So I told him. When I finished, he said, "I don't think it's safe for you to stay there with Mrs. Whitmore."

I threw my partly smoked cigarette out of the window. "I don't like the idea myself, but I seem to be stuck with it."

"Not necessarily. You can always change your mind. You could get a room at the inn. And I'm sure she would be glad to get rid of you."

"I believe she would. All of which whets my curiosity. Why? Why does she want to get rid of me? Why does everyone up here want to get rid of me? Is it because I'm a friend of Ed Harding?"

He put an arm around my shoulders and pulled me close to him, disposing of what was left of his cigarette in the car's ash tray on the dashboard. "*I* don't want to get rid of you." He kissed my cheek like a big brother. "And believe me, none of this would be of any interest to Ed Harding."

"I'm not so sure. There is something queer about the whole business," I said, enjoying the feel of his strong body so close to mine.

"That's for sure," he agreed.

"And I think you know what it is."

"Vaguely."

"Can't you tell me?"

"I could, but I think the less you know, the safer you are."

"Who had Mrs. Whitmore seen and talked to on the other side of the rocks?"

He hesitated before telling me, "Her stepson, Isaac."

"But why is he staying in one of the fishermen's shacks? Why doesn't he stay with her?"

"I guess she didn't even know he was here. He probably didn't want her to know."

"But that seems very strange." I thought about it for a moment, remembering the man who had taken my picture. "What does he look like?" I asked.

"Oh, sort of nondescript. Light hair. a mustache."

I bounded on the seat. "I've seen him!" I told him about driving up to and over the rocks, and about the man who had called to me and then snapped my picture.

"Sounds like something he would do. He's a queer duck."

"Would he do any of the things that have happened to me?"

"I wouldn't think so. But I wish you'd go home, just to be on the safe side."

I didn't have an answer for that, so we sat silently for a while, and I let my head rest against his shoulder. Cars came and went, stopping for a while to watch the gibbous moon on the restless waves below. It was peaceful there on the promontory, high above the sea, and I could have stayed there forever, close to David Carter's side.

Then suddenly his arm around me tightened, and his lips sought mine, found them, and for a blissful uncharted time, we clung together.

Finally he let me go, started the car and turned on the lights. "We'd better get back," he said.

As if nothing had happened, he backed the car, turned it around onto the road and drove back to the Whitmore place without saying another word.

Even though it wasn't yet ten o'clock, I got ready and crawled into bed, locking the door and putting out the lamp with reluctance. I had taken two of Dr. Cabot's pills, so I went to sleep almost immediately.

I was surprised to wake up and discover it was broad daylight. I looked at my watch. It was ten minutes to seven. I'd better get up. I did so and went over and looked out a window. Saban was puttering around in the aviary. He had on his black velvet Mohammendan hat and his gold hoop earrings, which looked silly to me. Mrs. Whitmore was fixing something at the back of the aviary. As usual, she was wearing slacks, a man's shirt and the gold hoop earrings. I couldn't help thinking they were a strange pair; completely alien to one another, yet in some ways similar.

I went into the bathroom, took a shower, came back to my room and dressed. I decided slacks and a blouse were the most suitable apparel for me, too. There was no way of knowing what the day would hold.

When I went down to breakfast, Mrs. Whitmore was just coming in from the kitchen. She said, "Good morning. Did you sleep well?"

I said, "Yes, thank you. And you?"

She shrugged. "I never sleep for a very long time."

We sat down at the table. At each place was a piece of cantaloupe. Mrs. Whitmore said, "I've been thinking – as long as you're here, you might as well paint some of the birds. I'd like a picture of several of them. That is, if you feel up to it."

Between mouthfuls of melon, I said, "Yes, I'm all right now. I'll get my things right after breakfast. Will it be all right for me to work inside the aviary?"

"Yes, if you don't mind the birds flying around over your head."

"I can try it. If they get in my way, maybe I can work from the outside."

Mrs. Whitmore helped me get settled in the aviary, suggesting the first bird I paint be her favorite, the one that was black with the large bifurcated shield of metallic greeny-blue feathers rising from his head and sweeping over his back.

At first my presence disturbed the birds, and there was quite a commotion and screeching, the like of which I'd never heard. But after a while when they found I wasn't going to harm them, they quieted down, and Mrs. Whitmore left me.

As I started to mix my paints, I realized

painting these birds was not going to be simple. Their colorings defied mere tubes of paint, and the best I could do was approximate.

For over an hour I worked steadily, directing all my attention to the bird I was trying to capture on my canvas. Saban had disappeared, and I began to sense I was alone in the big cage with the weird birds. Several of them eyed me with suspicion and occasionally screeched and squawked their disapproval of my presence.

When I began to tire, I laid down my brush and looked around. I would have liked to go over and examine the bowerbird's bower, but I dared not for fear I would cause too much commotion. From where I was sitting I could see the back of the bower, which looked like a beehive made of twigs. Dotted through it were bits of blue: a tiny blue flower, a bit of blue ribbon, a piece of something that looked like blue glass. I was intrigued and decided I'd ask Mrs. Whitmore about it later. There was no other color – only blue.

I turned back to my painting. It wasn't too bad. I'd caught the feeling of the bird and reproduced the metallic coloring as nearly as it could be done with paint.

I decided I'd done enough for a first sitting and, gathering up my materials with as little motion as I could, so I wouldn't frighten the birds, I got up, closed my paint box and my folding camp stool. Holding my wet canvas carefully so I wouldn't smear it. I walked toward the gate, only to find it locked. Well, it was natural enough for Mrs. Whitmore to keep her valuable collection of birds locked up. But *I* didn't like the idea of being locked up. And where was Mrs. Whitmore and Saban – or even Mary?

After a moment I could hear Mary clattering around in the kitchen, so I called, "Yoohoo, Mary!" But Mary was making so much noise banging pots and pans and dishes around, she couldn't hear me.

So I opened my camp stool and sat down, resting the wet canvas against the fence. Somebody would come along eventually. In the meantime, I could get a closer look at the bowerbird's bower. The inside of it seemed to be blackened. And even in the front, over the wide entrance opening, I could see small pieces of blue. I would have liked to go over and pull out one of the shiny pieces but didn't dare. The bowerbird himself was up in a nearby tree, making shrill whistling noises at me. Well, I could make a quick sketch of the bower while I was waiting to be set free. I had a piece of canvas board in the top of my paint box. So I quickly opened the box, mixed some paint, and in a few minutes I had a good sketch of the bower, blue dots and all. Then, up in the corner of the canvas board, I made a sketch of the bird himself. In his excitement he was frantically hopping around, so I never got a good look at him, but I managed to get a likeness nevertheless.

The sun was beginning to get hot, and I couldn't get into the shade without disturbing one or the other of the birds. Then my head began to ache. Carefully I felt of the lump on the back of my head. It was still there but wasn't so sore as it had been yesterday. I closed my paint box again and looked at my watch. It was eleven o'clock.

I was beginning to feel drowsy and leaned the side of my head against the wire mesh. I guess I was almost asleep when I heard a car come into the driveway. Instantly I was awake. Maybe it was David. I got up and walked over so I could see. It was only Lieutenant Cory. He got out of his car, and I called to him. For a moment he couldn't tell from where my voice was coming, so I called, "Back here! In the aviary."

He looked in my direction then and came back. With a big grin he asked, "What kind of a bird are you?"

"I guess I'm a whatsis."

"You have beautiful plumage."

"Thank you, kind sir. But do you suppose you could find someone to let me out of here?"

He laughed. "I can try," he said, turned and went toward the back door of the house.

In a moment Mrs. Whitmore came out. "Forgive me, my dear," she said. "I didn't mean to imprison you." She unlocked the gate, opened it and let me out. "How did it go?" she asked, relocking the gate. I showed her my partly finished painting of her favorite bird. As she looked at it, she nodded her head. "Very good," she said. "You've caught him very well."

I didn't mention the sketches I had made of the bowerbird and his bower. I said, "It's getting too hot to work any more today. I'll come out again tomorrow morning."

We went into the house together, and I noticed she hung the key on a nail near the kitchen door. Lieutenant Cory was talking to Mary. When we came in, they stopped. I thought Mrs. Whitmore looked annoyed. She said, "Come into the living room, Lieutenant Cory, please."

He bowed and followed her out of the kitchen, and I was right behind them. But in the hall I left them and went up to my room. I always like to clean my paint brushes and pallet as soon as I finish working. Also, I felt I'd like another shower and a change of clothing. I'd gotten quite warm sitting out there in the sun.

As I worked, I wondered if Mrs. Whitmore was going to tell Lieutenant Cory about Coral's disappearance, If she didn't, should I? Or should I just mind my own business?

I had just finished dressing in fresh underclothes and a yellow linen shift, with a yellow silk scarf tying back my hair, when Mary came upstairs. "Lunch is ready," she told me. "And David Carter is here. He wants to see you."

I said, "Thank you, Mary. Has Lieutenant Cory gone?"

"Yes, he's gone."

I took a chance and asked, "Mary, is something queer going on here?"

For a moment I thought she looked frightened, but she quickly covered it up. "Queer? I don't know what you mean."

"Don't you? Then why is Lieutenant Cory coming here?"

"Oh, that," she said, as if relieved. "That was about Mrs. Whitmore's jewels. Some of them are missing."

"Are they insured?"

"Oh, yes, ma'am. She's notified the insurance company. They're sending a man up from Boston. But first she had to tell the police."

"What does the insurance company do?"

She shrugged. "I suppose they work with the police. I wouldn't know. I ain't never had anything worth insuring."

"Nor I. But I suppose they have to make an investigation before they pay out money on a claim." I gave my hair an extra pat in front of the bureau mirror. "Well, I'm ready. Shall we go downstairs?"

David was waiting for me in the living room. When he saw me, he started to grin. "Your nose is red," he said.

"It is not!"

"Look at yourself." He led me over to an oval mirror between two windows. My nose *was* getting red. I hadn't noticed it upstairs. And freckles were starting to show on my cheeks. That's what comes of having red hair.

"I've been sitting in the sun," I told David.

"Oh?"

"Yes. I was in the aviary, painting one of the birds of paradise."

"You were?" He gave me a look that was a question. I knew what he meant. Had I been

126

snooping around, and if so, had I found out anything?"

I shook my head. "It's rather noisy out there," I said, "with all the birds screeching."

Suddenly I had an idea. I asked, "Is there a library around here anywhere?"

"A small one in the village. What do you want? Something to read?"

"No. I want to do some research."

"Oh? On what subject?"

"Birds. Bowerbirds specifically."

He raised his eyebrows. "Afraid I can't help you." He started to say something else, but just then I heard footsteps come through the hall from the back of the house. I shook my head at him and put a finger to my lips. Mrs. Whitmore appeared at the door to the living room. "Oh, there you are," she said. "Lunch is ready. Will you join us, David?"

He bowed. "I'd like to, if it won't be too much trouble."

"No trouble at all. We're having lobster salad, hot rolls and coffee. We don't bother much with lunch."

"Sounds wonderful," David said, and the three of us went out to the dining room. There were three places set at the table, and Mary was standing waiting for us. Seeing the extra place setting, David said, "Mary, you

127

must have ESP."

Mary grunted. "I don't know what that is. I just use the plain ordinary common sense the Lord gave me."

David laughed. "I get it. A man arrives to make a call just at mealtime. So what can the hostess do but invite him to stay. And when he's a lone bachelor who doesn't like to cook for himself – well, he accepts the invitation gratefully."

Mary grunted. "That's about it." She shuffled into the kitchen, and Mrs. Whitmore asked, "Come to think of it, what *do* you do about meals, David?"

He shrugged. "Oh, I have a grill out on the beach, and I toss a steak or a couple of hamburgers on it. If I get real hungry, I go in to the inn."

Mary came back with a tray on which were three plates of delicious-looking lobster salad. "Is that insurance man coming this afternoon?" she asked Mrs. Whitmore.

Mrs. Whitmore's lips tightened, and she looked as if she would have liked to tell Mary to shut up. But instead she said, "I don't know."

Mary placed a dish of salad before each of us. "Well, if he comes sometime and you ain't here, what'll I tell him?"

"Don't tell him anything. You don't know

128

anything about it."

"That's right. I don't." Mary shuffled back to the kitchen.

We each began to eat our salad. Then David said to me, "Feel like a ride this afternoon?"

I said, "Ride? Where to?"

He shrugged. "Oh, maybe we could make Rockport. They have a library there."

I gave Mrs. Whitmore a quick glance, but she seemed uninterested in the conversation between David and me.

Mary returned with a plate of hot rolls covered with a white damask napkin and began passing the plate around, lifting a corner of the napkin so each person could take a roll without letting the rest of them cool off. When Mrs. Whitmore reached out her hand to take a roll from beneath the napkin, Mary asked, "What you got that blue string on your ring for?"

Mrs. Whitmore gave her what could only be interpreted as a dirty look. "It's too big for me. I must have lost weight. I was afraid I'd lose it."

"Then why do you wear it?" Mary asked succinctly.

Tightening her lips, Mrs. Whitmore said, "You can bring the coffee now, Mary."

Mary returned the dirty look. "Yes,

ma'am," she said, set the plate of rolls on the table with a bang and returned to the kitchen.

David and I exchanged looks, and David said, "Would you like to join Jill and me this afternoon?" He looked at Mrs. Whitmore with an inviting smile.

She was buttering a piece of roll, and her hands were trembling. She said, "No, thank you, David. I think I'd better stay home, in case that insurance man does come. The claim is quite a large one, and I want it to go through as quickly as possible."

Mary brought in the coffee on a tray. "Saban's gone," she announced.

"Gone? What do you mean – gone?" Mrs. Whitmore snapped.

"I mean gone. G-o-n-e. Vamoosed. Bag and luggage."

Mrs. Whitmore dropped the piece of roll she was buttering. "But he can't *do* that!" she cried angrily.

Mary put a cup of coffee down beside each of us. "Well, he's done it," she said.

Mrs. Whitmore pushed her chair away from the table. "Where did he go?" she asked Mary.

"How do *I* know? He didn't tell me. He didn't even say goodbye. He just went out to his room over the garage, and then

I saw him come down with his bags and walk out to the road. And in a few minutes a car came along, and he got in it and went."

"Why didn't you tell me at once?"

"It just happened, while I was pouring out the coffee."

"What kind of a car was it?"

"I don't know. Just a car. I think it was black, but it was so dirty you couldn't tell."

"Who was in the car?"

"I couldn't see. A man."

David and Mrs. Whitmore exchanged glances, and Mrs. Whitmore asked, "Which way were they going?"

"The man came from the direction of Sand's End, and they went toward the village."

David asked, "Do you want me to call the police?"

Mrs. Whitmore stood up, leaving her partly eaten lunch. "No. It doesn't make any difference. Besides, what can the police do?" She left the dining room and went upstairs, and Mary returned to the kitchen.

David said, "Let's get out of here."

"But I haven't finished my lunch. And it's good."

He crumpled his napkin, put it beside his

131

plate and took a large gulp of coffee. "Well, we can get something on the road."

I said, "All right. Just a minute. I'll get my purse."

When I went upstairs, Mrs. Whitmore's door was closed. I got my purse and a sweater, in case it cooled off later; then I decided I'd pull down the shades to keep the hot afternoon sun out of the room. Just as I had my hand on the first one, I noticed Mrs. Whitmore in the aviary. She must have gone down the back stairs. She was puttering around the bowerbird's bower. The thought occurred to me that she spent a lot of time around the bower. I pulled down the shade and went downstairs. David was waiting for me in the hall. Without a word we went out of the house and got into his station wagon, which he'd left out on the road.

Chapter Eleven

While I was in the library, David did some shopping. He said he needed a few things he was unable to get in Pine Grove Harbor. We planned to meet in a little tearoom sort of place we'd passed down on the next block, with fishnet curtains at the windows and window boxes.

It took me a while to dig out anything about bowerbirds, but at last I found exactly what I wanted, and by the time I met David I was so excited I could scarcely talk. I'd written it all down on a piece of paper, and over a pot of tea and some dainty little sandwiches and homemade chocolate cake, I gave David the paper. On it I'd written:

> "... blue satin bowerbird ... will steal anything blue; blue flowers, feathers, bits of blue glass, and weave them into his bower ..."

David read it and gave it back to me with a smile. "So now you know. The little guy likes blue."

My hand was trembling as I took the paper and returned it to my purse. "Yes, now I know." I looked up at David. "Now I know where Mrs. Whitmore's jewels are."

"How so?"

"Don't you see? Blue! She had a blue string tied around her big diamond ring. And she didn't like it when Mary called attention to it."

We were sitting at a table besides an open window. David gazed out at the window box on the sill. It was full of petunias. "That's right: she didn't. But I still don't see —"

"I didn't tell you this, but when I went up to my room after lunch I looked out a window, and she had evidently gone down the back stairs after she'd left us at lunch and was fussing around the bowerbird's bower."

"So —"

"So I'd like to bet while she was fussing around out there, her diamond ring accidently slipped off, and now she can't find it."

David finished the sandwich he was eating. "What are you talking about? Do you know?"

I leaned my arms on the table so I could be closer to him. "Yes. Don't you see?"

"No." He began on the chocolate cake.

"Blue! The bowerbird will steal anything blue and weave it into his bower. So the jewels, probably one at a time, have been tied with blue in various ways, and put where the bowerbird would find them."

"And? This is good cake."

"And where no one would ever think of looking for them."

David stopped eating. Dawning comprehension began to spread over his face. "Well, I'll be darned! How could I be so stupid?"

I leaned back, ignoring his remark. "And probably by now, Mrs. Whitmore's diamond

134

ring has been found by the bowerbird and neatly tucked into the bower somewhere, with nothing but a bit of blue showing."

David lit a cigarette. "I don't believe it. It's too fantastic!"

"That's why she is getting away with it."

"But the insurance company isn't that dumb."

"Of course they aren't dumb. But I don't suppose they would make a search for the jewels, and even if they did they would only search the house."

"I don't think they would even do that. I guess they have to take people's word for it. And if they pay the claim, she can't ever insure those particular jewels again, because they will have a description of them. Nor can she wear them. But as I understand it, some of them are uncut stones. Her husband had quite a valuable collection, and when he died she took them."

"And each one could be wrapped in blue paper or tied with blue ribbon or string."

David looked at me thoughtfully. "I wonder if Saban knows?"

"He must know the habits of the bowerbirds. They live in his native country."

"Could they be in cahoots, she and Saban?"

"They could be. I wonder if Saban took any

135

of the jewels with him."

"She was very upset last night when I told her Saban had been cleaning up around the bower, and that was what had disturbed the birds."

"Yes, she was. And now today, Saban goes away."

"But even if all this is true, it doesn't explain Coral's murder, or the things that happened to you out at Sand's End."

"No. But I can't help feeling they are all related."

David said, "Um."

"Should we tell Lieutenant Cory about the bowerbird's passion for blue?"

He shrugged. "It's really none of our business. And you've had trouble enough. My suggestion to you is to go home right away. If you don't feel up to driving, go on the train. I'll drive your car down for you later. I'll be in New York after Labor Day. I have an apartment on East 35th Street."

I watched a small black bug taking a stroll on a white petunia. "I can't just walk out on the whole mess."

"Why not? None of it has anything to do with you."

"Have the police made a search of the fishermen's shacks on the other side of the rocks out at Sand's End?"

"I don't know."

"Don't you think they should?"

He smiled at me and finished the chocolate cake, then took a puff on his cigarette. "I'm not going to start telling the police what to do. Besides, if Isaac is over there – well, it's none of our business. It's a family affair, and there are things it's a good idea not to get mixed up with."

I began to feel defeated. David was right: it was none of my business. Yet I had been so much involved in it I couldn't help feeling very much a part of it. I said, "Let's start back. Maybe we can make it before dark."

He put out his cigarette and picked up the check that the waitress had left beside his plate. "I doubt it," he said. "It's after five now, and we will have to stop somewhere for dinner."

We got up from the table. "We don't have to bother with dinner," I said.

He put an arm around me and propelled me toward a woman sitting behind a cash register that was on a table near the door. "We are going to stop for a nice shore dinner on the way back. And don't give me any back talk." He gave me a hug and paid the check, and we went onto the street. It was still quite warm. As we walked to where the car was parked in front of the library, David took my arm. "Somebody has to take care of you while you're up here on the rocky coast of Maine. And you can't go without food." He grinned. "Anyway, if you can, I can't. In about an hour I'm going to be starved."

I smiled up at him. "You're nice, David," I said. "And I'll take your advice about stopping for dinner. But I am not going home until I find out what is going on down at Pine Grove Harbor and Sand's End."

He looked serious at that. "And if you ever do find out, you may not live long enough to get home."

"I wish you'd tell me what you know."

"No. You know too much all ready."

He drove back as fast as he could all the way, but he did insist on stopping at a very attractive sea food place right on the water in a little cove where they served us a delicious shore dinner. And he also insisted I eat all of it, and take my time doing it. So it was nearly midnight by the time we got back to the Whitmore place.

There was a light in the hall, and Mary was waiting up for us, but she had gotten undressed and was in her bathrobe and slippers, her hair in a long braid hanging over one shoulder. I guess she'd been lying

138

down on the brown plush sofa in the living room, because when she heard us come in, she appeared at the door, yawning. "Where you been? I got worried?" she said in a loud whisper.

I whispered back, "You needn't have stayed up."

"I couldn't go to bed and leave the door unlocked." She scratched one hip and yawned again. "Besides, something awful's happened."

"Awful? What?" David asked.

"The police were here. They've found Coral's body – or what's left of it!"

I could feel myself waver and grabbed at David's arm.

"Where's Au – Mrs. Whitmore?" he asked.

"Up in bed. She's very upset."

"I should think she would be," I said, and my voice sounded far away.

David asked, "Had I better go up and see her?"

Mary scratched her hip. "No. Wouldn't do no good. Can't do anything before morning. Then somebody has to go to the morgue and identify her."

I shuddered, and David put an arm around me. To Mary he said, "I'd better stay here for the night. I can sleep on the sofa in the living room."

139

Mary sighed. "That wouldn't do no good. Done's done. Come back for breakfast if you want. There'll probably be a big to-do tomorrow."

David thought that over for a while, then said, "Well, I guess you're right. I'll get here early." Then, turning to me, "Be sure and lock your door."

I just nodded, and he turned and went out.

After he'd gone Mary locked the front door. "You go up first," she said, "then I'll put out the light down here. I lit a lamp in your room."

I said, "Thank you, Mary."

As soon as my aching head was laid, as gently as I could lay it, on the soft down pillow, I fell asleep, and that was all I remembered until something awakened me.

Something was going on out back in the aviary. I lay still and tense, listening. Above the noise all the other birds were making, the shrill call of the bowerbird could be heard. He sounded frightened, frantic!

I jumped out of bed and ran to a window. It was a very dark night. Either the moon had already risen and set or it hadn't yet risen. We hadn't seen it on our drive back from Rockport, and it was not shining now.

Straining my eyes, I tried to see into the aviary. I could hear the flutter of the wings of the excited birds, but there was no other sound. I listened, holding my breath. Yes, there was another sound, like cracking twigs. And a very small pencil-like light was being passed over the bower of the bowerbird.

Suddenly I had to know what was going on. I put on my slippers and grabbed my raincoat. I'd brought up only one robe, my light blue cloth, so now I didn't have one.

I opened my door and listened. Surely Mrs. Whitmore must have heard the commotion out in the aviary. I didn't know which side of the house Mary's room was on. All I knew was that she was on the third floor somewhere.

Quickly running down the stairs, through the big square front hall and into the kitchen, I fumbled for the nail on which I'd seen Mrs. Whitmore hang the key to the aviary. At last I found it, but the key was gone. My heart gave a jerk. Maybe it was she out in the aviary. If so, I had nothing to fear. Or did I? If she was collecting her jewels from their clever hiding place in the bowerbird's bower, would she want me to discover her? And if I did, to what lengths would she go to silence me?

I sidled over to the door out to the back porch and found it ajar. Carefully I went down the steps and crept across the grass to the aviary. Now I could see a dark mass

141

bending over the bower. The gate was wide open. Whoever was there was too busy to notice my approach, but the birds could see me, or sense me, and they screeched even louder.

I crept closer to the bower, and as my eyes became accustomed to the darkness I could distinguish the form of a man. He was carefully tearing the bower apart, twig by twig, and when his probing fingers would find something he was searching for, he would slip it into his pocket.

Something flew over my head. It looked and sounded like the ghost bird Mary had told me about, and its long tail feathers flicked my face. I shuddered and drew away just as a shot whizzed past my right cheek. The man dismantling the bower cried out, then crashed down on top of the bower with a groan, accompanied by the sound of cracking twigs and the screeching of the bowerbird, which was now deafening.

The shot had come from behind me, and I whirled around, to be confronted by Mrs. Whitmore holding a rifle. I gasped and backed away from her.

"Get in the house!" she ordered me.

For a moment I couldn't speak or move. Then I asked, in a small shaky voice, "Shall I call the police?"

She pointed the rifle at my face. "If you do I'll blow your head off!" she said. I would have expected her to scream at me, but she didn't. She spoke quietly but firmly.

I walked past her out of the aviary and over to the house, up the steps to the back porch and into the kitchen. By the time I reached the front hall, Mary was hurrying down the stairs, putting on her robe as she came. "What's the matter?" she asked me. She'd snapped on a light as she came along the second floor hall, and she could see me by that.

I managed to get to a chair before my knees gave way. "Out back," I said. "In the aviary. I think Mrs. Whitmore has shot a man."

"Oh, God almighty!" Mary cried. Having now reached the bottom of the stairs, she swung herself around the newel post and began to run toward the kitchen.

But I called, "Wait! Don't go out there. She's got a rifle. She threatened to blow my head off if I called the police."

Mary turned around and stared at me. After a moment she asked, "Who did she shoot?"

I shook my head. "I couldn't see. It was too dark. But he was tearing the bowerbird's bower apart."

Mary tied the cord of her robe around her
143

thick waist. "Why was he doing that?"

"Can't you guess?"

I could see she was trembling now. It was rather chilly there in the hall, and with the kitchen door open there was a cool night breeze blowing in from the back. I put my arms into the raincoat I'd thrown around my shoulders when I'd gone outside and buttoned it down the front.

Mary stood watching me. "How can I guess?" she asked me, a look of bewilderment in her faded blue eyes.

"The bowerbird likes blue. Mrs. Whitmore had blue string tied around her ring . . ."

Mrs. Whitmore appeared in the kitchen doorway. She had on a pair of gray slacks and a pull-over sweater. Her feet were bare. She pointed the rifle at me. "That will be enough!" she said, her face taut, her lips tight.

Mary turned and looked at her. Quietly she said, "Put down that gun, Agnes." Then she added, "You old fool!"

Agnes Whitmore looked at her. The point of the gun was lowered and rested on the floor, and I expelled a sigh of relief. She said, "I've just killed Isaac." Suddenly her shoulders slumped. "He killed Coral, and now I've killed him." She walked over and propped the gun in a niche beneath the stairs.

"I guess that does it," she added wearily.

Mary and I were holding our breath. At least I was holding mine. But neither of us spoke. We just watched a very old woman walk across the hall and drag herself up the stairs with the aid of the bannister rail. I noticed she wasn't wearing either her gold hoop earrings or the big diamond ring.

When she had disappeared from our sight and we'd heard the door to her room close, Mary went over to the phone. I said, "Don't call the police. She doesn't want them to know."

Mary picked up the phone. "I'm not calling the police," she told me. "I'm calling David Carter."

I stared at her. "David Carter? But why him – now?"

Mary's mouth tightened. "You'll find out," she told me grimly, and picked up the phone. He must have been asleep, because it took him a while to answer. When he did Mary said, "David, it's Mary. Come quickly! Agnes has just shot Isaac!"

I sat there in the drafty hall listening. I couldn't have moved if my life had depended on it. Or at least I thought I couldn't, until I saw the man standing in the kitchen doorway with a menacing-looking gun in his hand. It was black and stubby and very ugly. He said

145

to Mary. "Put down that phone!" He was of medium height, with broad shoulders, a thick neck and torso. He had sun-streaked light brown hair, rather shaggy, and in the dim light his eyes looked colorless. I guess they were some kind of blue. And he had a mustache, droopy and long at the ends. He was dressed in dirty brown corduroy trousers, a soiled light blue plaid shirt and a black suede jacket covered with dirt, and blood was rapidly staining his shirt and running down beneath the jacket onto his trousers. He was the man I'd seen on the other side of the rocks, the one who had snapped my picture.

Mary dropped the phone and whirled around. "Isaac!" she said, scarcely above a whisper. "We thought you were dead!"

He smiled, or leered would be a better word, and what teeth showed were stained brown, I guess from chewing betel root. Apparently, though English, he had gone completely native in New Guinea. He said, "Thought or hoped?" He took a step toward Mary, and she backed up until she was against the wall. "Where is Agnes?" he demanded.

"She's upstairs," Mary stammered.

Isaac started for the stairs, jabbing Mary viciously with his elbow as he passed her. Then he staggered and would have fallen if I hadn't jumped up and caught him, holding

146

him with both arms. But it was all I could do to keep him up. He was too heavy for the small amount of strength I had left, and I must have jogged his gun hand, because there was the sound of a shot, and I felt him go limp as he sagged to the floor. Mary screamed, and I knelt down beside him. But before I could see whether or not he was dead, a high-pitched man's voice said, "You go away, Mem Sahib!"

I looked up into the face of Saban. He was holding a rifle, and his black velvet Mohammedan hat was tipped over his forehead at a rakish angle. I couldn't be sure, but I thought he was drunk.

I gasped and managed to get to my feet, my breath rushing in and out of my lungs so fast it was smothering me. "Saban!" I cried. "You shot him! You've *killed* him!"

He grinned then, and his two gold teeth showed as he stood there in the kitchen doorway with the smoking gun in his hand. "He dead – I hope." With a nonchalant movement he came and gave me his rifle and knelt down beside Isaac, flung him over on his back so his horrible distorted face showed, then got up and gave the dead man a kick in the ribs. "He dead," he said with satisfaction. "Me – I keel him! He keel Mem Sabib Coral – I keel him."

147

I stared at him. "But Coral was his daughter!" I protested.

He nodded, and the black velvet Mohammedan hat wobbled. "She his daughter but she my girl. I make love with her."

"You lie, Saban!" It was Mrs. Whitmore, coming slowly down the stairs. She stopped halfway and leaned on the bannister, looking down at the tableau we made in the hallway below her.

Saban looked up at her. "No lie, Tuan."

"Yes, you do. You'd have liked to make love with her, but she'd never let you!"

He shook his head, and his hands, hanging at his sides now, were clenched into fists. "I make love with her," he said. "I honest man. I want to make marry with her, but she say she just want make love with me. She say she want make marry with white man, be United States ceetzen."

Mrs. Whitmore's face seemed to have aged ten years since breakfast. "Then *you* probably killed her, instead of Isaac."

Saban went over to the stairs and looked up into Mrs. Whitmore's face. "No! Not true! Tuan Isaac keeled her. He thought she was that one." He jerked his head toward me.

I cried. "Oh! But why *me?*"

148

Saban turned around. "Because you in way. He want beach by shack for landing boat."

"Boat? What boat?" I asked, suddenly realizing I was shaking from head to foot. "I never saw a boat. Not on my side of the rocks."

"He have leetle boat an' go out to beeg boat, an' he can't do it on beach where fishermen are. He no want fishermen to know he get white powder from beeg boat way out. So he want your beach. He try to scare you away, but you not get scared."

I stared at him. "Then it was he who tried to drown me by pulling me under the water when I was swimming?"

Saban nodded. "He got diving things. he swim under water a long time."

"And it was he that night, with the masks and the arrows?"

Saban nodded again. "He got boys and girls from fishermen families and tell them they make party on your beach and wear spirit masks and dance around fire and beat drums and have fun."

"You mean it was boys and girls who shot arrows at me and hit me on the back of the head and then pinned me down to the beach with arrows?"

"No, Mem Sahib. He do that. When boys and girls see him hit you, they got scared and

149

ran away, and *he* pin you down on beach."

"But two people shot arrows at me when I was in the doorway."

Saban nodded. "I one. I good shot with bow and arrow." Then he grinned and gave the dead Isaac another kick. "And with gun," he added. He kept grinning. "I try to scare you away, too, so he not get you." Then he dropped down on his knees and began going through Isaac's pockets, taking out pieces of uncut precious stones, several rings, among them the large diamond ring I had seen Mrs. Whitmore wearing, and a diamond pin. Each had a bit of blue tied to it.

With a cry Mrs. Whitmore came rushing down the stairs and grabbed up the jewels, putting them into the pockets of her trousers. Through clenched teeth she said, "Saban, I could slit your throat!"

Saban just grinned. "You no do that," he told her almost gleefully. "You geeve me half. I take good care of you. I not let Mem Sahib Coral keel you."

Mrs. Whitmore glared at him. "What do you mean? Coral didn't want to kill me."

"Yes, she did. That why she come way over here. She mean to keel you and get your money and the jewels, and marry some white man."

"I don't believe you."

150

"I tell the truth. So you geeve me half the jewels."

"I'll do no such thing! I'll have you arrested."

Heavy footsteps came up the front porch, and someone hammered on the door. Mrs. Whitmore was nearest to it and unlocked and opened it, and David, Lieutenant Cory and Sergeant Kelly came in. The three men looked at first one and then the other of us. Suddenly I realized I was standing there holding Saban's rifle, and at my feet was the dead Isaac. If ever there was a piece of circumstantial evidence, this was it.

After a moment of stunned silence, David strode over to me and took the rifle away from me. "Jill!" he cried. "For God's sake! What have you done?"

Lieutenant Cory came in and picked up Isaac's ugly little black gun that had slipped from his hand when he'd fallen.

Sergeant Kelly closed the door and stood by it as if on guard.

Mrs. Whitmore said, "Who sent for the police?" She looked accusingly at me.

No one spoke. I just shook my head.

"Did *you*, Mary? she demanded.

Mary said, "No. I just called David."

David said, "I brought them. And from the looks of things, it's a good thing I did."

151

Lieutenant Cory began to examine Isaac. He looked up at me. "Did you kill him?" he asked, a look of surprise in his eyes.

I shook my head. "No."

"But you had the gun."

"I – I –" I glanced over at Saban, and he grinned. Proudly he said, "I keel him. He no good."

Lieutenant Cory turned Isaac over, and a look of puzzlement replaced the look of surprise on his face. "He's been shot twice," he said, "once in the front and once in the back." He got to his feet and looked from one to the other of us; then he spotted the rifle Mrs. Whitmore had left standing in the niche in the back of the hall. He went over and picked it up. "Seems like you got a young arsenal here," he said. "It's a wonder you aren't all dead."

I couldn't help asking, "Saban, if you knew Coral was a bad girl, how could you love her?"

He shrugged. "Bad girl – good girl – got nothing to do with making love. She make good love."

I felt a chill creep up my back, making me even colder than I was already.

Lieutenant Cory went to the phone, and Mrs. Whitmore asked, "What are you going to do, Bill?"

"Call homicide and Dr. Cabot and an ambulance. You can't leave him just lying here."

"Who are you going to accuse of killing him?" Her voice had lost its commanding tone.

Lieutenant Cory made his calls and hung up the phone. Then he came back to stand near where Isaac lay. "There are three guns and four people who could have used them." He looked at me, at Saban, at Mary and at Mrs. Whitmore. "I guess it will have to be a process of elimination," he said. "Fingerprints, report from ballistics when they take the slugs out of him, things like that." He shoved his hat over his forehead and scratched the back of his head.

As I stood there shivering, I thought, Dear God – wait until Ed Harding hears about this.

Chapter Twelve

It didn't take long for the police to find out the truth. As a matter of fact, it all came out at the inquest, principally because all of us were only too anxious to tell the truth. Each and every one believed what he or she had done

153

was perfectly justified.

However, neither the police nor the insurance company believed Mrs. Whitmore had been justified in hiding her precious stones and jewelry in the bowerbird's bower and then asking the insurance company to pay her. If she had wanted to hide the stones where her step-granddaughter and her stepson couldn't find them, all well and good. That was her own business. But it was not a good idea to try to cheat a large insurance company. To be sure, she hadn't yet received any money from the insurance company, but they could at least get her on attempted fraud. However, that case would come up later.

As to me, I was only too glad to get away as soon as it was all over. I had found it difficult to sit through all the testimony at the inquest. Saban had been the principal witness, and he was more than willing to talk. He had said that Isaac had told him he had killed his daughter by mistake. He had been prowling around the beach late in the evening and had seen the girl near the shack and thought she was I, so he had crept up behind her and killed her. Then he saw it was Coral and she had a lot of jewelry with her. So he'd taken it away from her. Which explained the little metal box. Coral had evidently been stealing her grandmother's jewelry and hiding it in

154

the metal box, which she'd kept buried back of my outhouse. She must have come out to get it before leaving for Boston, and that was when her father had killed her. Then he had seen me find the body early that morning, and when I went away to notify the police he had hidden the body among the rocks until night. Then he went to find Saban and ask him to help him dispose of the body. They had tied a few rocks to it, taken it out in Isaac's small boat and thrown it overboard. But apparently, in their hurry and excitement, they hadn't tied the weights on tightly enough, and the beating of the waves and the pull of the tide had loosened the ropes. And eventually the body, or what was left of it, had risen to the surface and been washed up on the island beach. When Saban was questioned about why he helped Isaac dispose of the body of the girl he loved, he just shrugged. "She dead," he said. "She no more good. Tuan Isaac geeve me much money." He shrugged again. As far as he was concerned, he had done no harm.

The fishermen's shacks had been searched, and in one, at the very end of the row nearest the rocks, they had found Isaac's scuba diving suit and the devil masks. He always went in for tribal customs. They also found several quivers of arrows and several bows. And they found my paintings of Coral and David, which they returned to me. Also, under a loose floor board they found several pounds of heroine, which was the reason Isaac wanted to be unseen when he went out to the big boats in his small one. The thing that chilled me most was the fact that they had found the snapshot Isaac had taken of me in his pocket.

I didn't see David after the inquest. He had driven off in his station wagon, and Mary and I drove back to the Whitmore place in my car. Mrs. Whitmore was released on bail, but she would eventually have to stand trial for the attempted fraud. The fact that she had shot Isaac was made light of, because he was attempting to rob her.

As to Saban, he was kept in jail. He was the one who had actually killed Isaac. That fact was established without a doubt from the bullet found in Isaac's body.

Mrs. Whitmore drove home alone from the inquest in her Land-Rover, and later, over sandwiches and coffee, I told her I had decided to go home right away. She just shrugged. "The sooner the better, as far as I am concerned," she said ungraciously.

I didn't say goodbye to David. Maybe I'd write him later. But now I just wanted to get away. Anyway, he had never said he loved me, or even liked me. He had kissed me a few times and been nice to me, but that was nothing for a girl to pin her hopes on. Besides, Ed Harding would be back from his trip by now, and after what I'd been through on the rocky cost of Maine, I was going to be glad to see Ed.

So I packed my bag and said goodbye to Mrs. Whitmore and Mary and left late in the afternoon. I would send a check to Joe for the ice and to Dr. Cabot for the visit I'd made to his office.

I drove through the town of Pine Grove Harbor without stopping and headed for Boston, where I stayed the night. But I didn't do much sleeping. I kept thinking of David – of how wonderful it would have been if we had met under more favourable circumstances. I'd never realized I'd had an ideal man for whom I'd been waiting until I'd seen David. And then he was *it*. But I probably would never see him again, unless I was called back to testify in Saban's trial for the murder of Isaac, and Mrs. Whitmore's trial for attempted fraud. The prospect was unpleasant, and I shivered. I didn't really want to have any part in the conviction of either of them.

It was a relief to reach New York the following afternoon, even though the thermometer was registering around ninety. No longer did I want isolation and quiet. Now I craved people – the noise of the city – the jangle of the phone – Ed Harding.

He had just returned from his trip when I called him and was only too glad to take me to dinner.

I had never bothered to dress up too much for Ed, but tonight I was going really to do a job of it. So I put on a white pleated sheath dress with a wide gold belt, gold sandals and heavy gold jewelry. I brushed out my shoulder length auburn hair so it fell in soft swirls about my face. I put just enough shadow around my amber-colored eyes to make them look darker than they were, and I used a light-colored irridescent lipstick.

When Ed arrived at my studio apartment on East Tenth Street, he took me in his arms and kissed me, and I let him, trying to be glad to be back in the safety of his arms. But something was missing. All I could think of was David and David's kisses.

Ed noticed my unresponsiveness and stopped kissing me, held me at arm's length. "You've changed," he said. "What's happened?"

Ed was tall and well built, with short brown hair and intense brown eyes. His features were good, but when he was annoyed his lips became a mere line between his lean cheeks.

Tonight he was wearing a light tan summer suit, with a white shirt and a blue tie, and there was no denying he looked attractive. But comparing him to David, I couldn't feel enthusiastic about him.

I realized I was being silly, because Ed thought a lot more of me than David did. And he worked hard for a living and didn't just loaf around remote beaches.

I looked up at him and tried to smile, but I felt more like crying. Taking his hand, I led him over to the sofa, and we sat down. "I want to tell you a story," I said. Now that it was all over up in Maine, I felt I owed Ed an explanation. As I talked he listened intently, his newspaper-trained mind figuring all the angles. A couple of times he asked a question.

When I finished he asked, "Could you describe that man in the blue coupé to me?"

I said, "Yes. Better still, I have a charcoal sketch of him. Wait; I'll get it." I jumped up, and went into the big room I used for a studio and where I'd put my painting materials and the few sketches I'd made up in Maine when I got home. I picked up the sketch pad and took it in to Ed, holding it so he could see it. He studied it for a moment; then he began to smile. "Know who that looks like?" he asked.

"Like a gangster."

"Yes, he does look something like one. But

159

he's really more of a lamb. It's the image of Sid Granville of Granville and Block, the publishers. He got that scar on his cheek in the Second World War."

I drew in a surprised breath, "Oh, it couldn't be Sid Granville. He'd never write a note like that, with a skull and crossbones, and then pin it to the table with a knife!"

Ed grinned. "Want to bet? He loves doing things like that. You know the kind of books Granville and Block publish, don't you?"

"They specialize in murder mysteries, don't they?"

"Yes. What did the other fellow look like?"

I got up and went back to my studio and returned with my portrait of David. "Like this," I said, holding it up.

Ed tilted back his head and laughed.

"What's so funny?" I demanded, beginning to feel rather foolish.

Ed, still laughing, asked, "Don't you know who that is?"

"His name is David Carter."

"Yes, it is. But that is his real name. He writes under the name of Peter Lindy."

"Writes?"

"Sure. You ought to know. You read all his gory stories."

"But –" Still holding the portrait of David, I sank down on the nearest chair, feeling

160

suddenly weak. "Then he isn't just a beachcomber?"

"A beachcomber? Peter Lindy? Good heavens, no! He must be a millionaire – the way he turns out that crap he writes and then sells most of it to the movies and TV." Ed couldn't seem to stop laughing at me, and I suddenly hated him – his arrogance, his enjoyment of my discomfort. I said, "But no one up in Maine knows he is Peter Lindy. They only know him as David Carter."

"I don't know anything about that. All I know is he is a prolific writer of trash and is making a fortune on it."

"So?" I asked defiantly. Then I added, "He doesn't like you. Nobody up there likes you. And they were scared to death you'd come up there to visit me."

Ed smiled sardonically. "What have they got to hide?"

I slumped in my chair and put the portrait of David to one side. "I guess it's all out in the open now."

Ed stubbed out the remains of his cigarette and lit a fresh one. I asked, "What did you ever do to David?"

Ed shrugged. "Oh, that. Well, he had a kid sister. She joined the Peace Corps and was sent over to some outlandish place in Africa."

"So?"

161

"Well, she got herself mixed up with a tribal prince who had been over here to college, then gone back to help his people. The girl, being young, foolish and vulnerable, fell in love with the guy. He was good-looking and spoke good English. But he didn't want to do anything but play around. He was betrothed to a girl who was a princess of another tribe, and he was just having a little fun with Edith."

"So what business was it of yours?" I demanded.

He shrugged. "It was a good story. Romantic. Timely. So I investigated and wrote it up." He shrugged again. When the article was published and Edith read it, she committed suicide. Took an overdose of sleeping pills."

"And?"

"And Peter Lindy came after me and beat me up. That was before I knew you."

I sighed. "I vaguely remember the story. You made the Peace Corps sound like a den of iniquity and got called up before an investigating committee in Washington."

Ed smiled ruefully. "It wasn't the first time."

I stood up. "There may be a last time, Ed. Why don't you quit while you're ahead?"

"But, honey, it's my job. That's the way I

162

make my living. Is it any worse than writing that crap your friend Peter Lindy writes?"

I met his eyes defiantly. "Yes. At least the crap, as you call it, doesn't hurt anybody – except the fictional characters in the books."

"Oh, for heaven sakes!" Ed snapped. "Stop being so dramatic. Can't you see the funny side of it?"

"No, I can't. Nothing that happened to me up there in Maine was funny. Now please go and leave me alone."

Ed looked surprised. "I don't get it," he said. "What are you so upset about? You didn't even know any of those people a couple of weeks ago. Snap out of it.

"Come on; we'll go out to dinner and forget the whole thing."

"Forget it? I'll never forget it! And if you dare write one single word about what I've told you –!"

"Don't worry. That's small-time stuff. I have bigger fish to fry now. I didn't tell you where I was going this last trip because it was top secret. But I've just come back from Israel."

"So now you're going to tar and feather *them?*"

He got up and came over to me. "Oh, come off it, Jill," he said, taking hold of my shoulders. "Come on; marry me, as soon as

163

we can make the arrangements. You can't keep up that rat race you call a career. You'll wreck yourself. As soon as I write this Israeli story, we'll go to some nice gay place for a honeymoon. Maybe Paris. Then, while I'm in the Far East this fall, you can take your time getting a home together for us. Maybe we can buy a brownstone, or a co-op apartment?"

That did it. That completed the circle. I was right back where I'd started from. Ed meant well, as far as I was concerned, and he loved me - next to himself. But it was just no go for me.

I shook my head, and there were tears in my eyes. I said, "Thanks, Ed, but no thanks."

His hands dropped from my shoulders, and his eyes narrowed. Now he looked like the man who could tear people's lives apart with the tapping of his typewriter keys. His lips thinned, and his jaw tensed. "I'm getting tired of you, doll," he snapped at me. "If you send me away tonight, I'm not coming back."

I sighed. I knew he meant what he said, and if I sent him away tonight I wouldn't have anybody. David, although he'd kissed me a few times, didn't really want me. He'd even gone out of his way to fool me so he'd get rid of me - not telling me he was Peter Lindy when he'd seen me with one of his books, and letting me think Sid Granville and his silly note were dangerous to me. Some fun!

But with all that, I knew now I could never marry Ed Harding. I said, "I'm sorry, Ed, but that's the way it's going to be."

After he'd gone and I was in bed, completely unable to sleep, I wasn't sorry I'd turned Ed down once and for all. Yet the more I thought about David, the madder I got. He had played tricks on me, had he? Well, I wasn't going to let him get away with it.

About four o'clock in the morning, I decided I was going to go right back up there and tell him what I thought of him. And I'd never read another Peter Lindy book again as long as I lived.

I got up, showered, had some breakfast, and put on a green celanese sleeveless dress, a comfortable old pair of loafers, packed one bag with my night things and one extra dress and another pair of shoes. At six o'clock I went around to the all-night garage where I kept my car.

Chapter Thirteen

I reached Pine Grove Harbor late in the afternoon, went right through the village and out to David's house. It was wide open, and there was a car in the driveway – the blue coupé I'd seen once before – and in the garage was David's station wagon. I could hear voices, men's voices, coming from what must be the living room. I used a brass knocker, not too gently, and to my surprise, Mary came to the door. "Oh," she said, "it's you. Come in."

I said, "Hello, Mary. What are you doing here?" She looked tired, and she had aged just since yesterday. She sighed. "Oh, more trouble. Go on in. He'll tell you. He's in there."

I entered a large hall and looked around. To the right was a large, book-lined room. David and Sid were standing before a cobblestone fireplace, each holding a partly filled highball glass.

Entering the room, I asked, "May I come in?"

David put his glass on the mantel over the fireplace and crossed the room to meet me.

166

"I'm glad you came back," he said. Like Mary, he looked tired.

"Are you?" I asked. "Why?"

"Mrs. Whitmore had a stroke last night. She's in the hospital and has asked for you."

"Me? Why?"

"I guess she likes you. And she's all alone now. She hasn't anyone left but me."

I felt tears come to my eyes. "I'm sorry," I said. "I'll go to see her right away." But as I turned to leave, David caught my arm. "No, wait. I'll come with you. But first I want you to meet a friend of mine."

I looked over at Sid, and he smiled and bowed. Before David could introduce us, I said, "How do you do, Mr. Granville."

Both David and Sid looked surprised; then Sid asked, "You know who I am?"

I said, "Yes. I finally solved the mystery. You see, I know all the tricks. I read Peter Lindy's books from cover to cover. I just wasn't smart enough to recognize his master hand in the note and knife setup over at the shack."

Sid smiled. "And how did you eventually solve the mystery?"

"I'd drawn a picture of you, from memory, and I showed it to a friend of mine. Ed Harding. He recognized you. He also recognized a painting I'd done of –" I

167

hesitated – "David – I mean Peter Lindy."

David looked embarrassed. He said, "I'm sorry, Jill. I didn't want you to know."

"Why?"

"Well, because nobody up here knows I'm Peter Lindy. They know I write something, but they never paid any attention to *what*. If they knew I was Peter Lindy, they'd be shocked." He smiled ruefully.

"Even Mrs. Whitmore?"

"Particularly her."

Feeling instantly defensive for him, I said, "There is nothing to be shocked about. What you write is good stuff. I enjoy it."

He grinned. "Thank you," he said. "May I give you a drink?"

I said, "No, thank you. I'll be going along to the hospital, and then I'll get a room at the inn." I turned to Sid. "But before I go, I would like to know why you came out to my shack that day."

David answered for him. "He thought I was still there. I hadn't let him know I'd moved, because I knew if he found me, he'd start hounding me again." He smiled slightly. "That's why I left my apartment down in New York – to get away from him."

I was beginning to piece that part of the story together. "And when he saw some of your clothes in the closet with mine –"

168

"Exactly," David said, "although he should have known me better than that."

"And the note with the knife stuck in it?"

"The note was a joke, of course," David explained. "Sid and I always write each other notes like that. And when I discovered you read my books, I thought it would be amusing to try to make you think you were living one of my stories. I thought maybe you'd get a kick out of it. Also, I really didn't want to be disturbed by anyone in the immediate neighborhood. Sid has been on my neck, trying to get me to turn out books faster than it is humanly possible. So I haven't had time for any social life. But when I saw you, I knew if you were around I was going to want to see you. So I had to get rid of you, if I was going to meet the deadlines Sid had set up for me."

I could hear the swish of the sea outside the windows, and the screech of the gulls as they circled for their intermittent dives into the waves for their supper. I said, "I suppose it was silly of me to be frightened. But I'd been working rather hard myself, and my nerves were a bit on edge. And then when all those other things began happening –"

"I think we owe the young lady our humble apology," Sid told David.

David nodded. "Of course. We didn't mean to frighten you. And then, with the other

169

things that happened to you out there – it was a very bad joke. I am truly sorry. So is Sid."

Surprised they hadn't laughed at me, the way Ed had, I glanced from one to the other. Sid wasn't as bad-looking as I'd thought. His eyes were kind, and he had a nice smile. He finished his drink and put the empty glass on the mantel. "Well," he said, "I'll go along. I want to make Boston tonight. And you two want to go over to the hospital."

After he'd gone, David took my hand, led me over to a large man-sized sofa opposite the fireplace, and we sat down side by side. "I really am sorry," he said. "But I do wish you had gone home that day Sid left the note. It would have saved you all the rest of it." He still had hold of my hand.

"But if I had – well, we wouldn't have gotten to know each other."

He smiled. "That's right; we wouldn't have. But some day I would have come looking for you, because I knew the moment I laid eyes on you, standing there in the moonlight, the night you arrived, that you were the girl I'd been waiting for."

I felt my cheeks flush, and when he took me in his arms and kissed me I just closed my eyes and let ecstasy rush over me. When the kiss was finished, I said, "But you let me go away."

He smiled and touched my lips with a forefinger. "I didn't let you. You just went – without saying goodbye."

My eyes met his, and I smiled. "I came back," I pointed out.

He took both my hands. "If you hadn't, I'd have come after you. That is if – well, maybe you'd rather have your friend, Ed Harding?"

I shook my head. "No, that's over." Then I added. "I'm sorry about your sister. He told me about it."

David's hands tightened. "I nearly killed him," he said. "The dirty swine!"

I said, "I'm terribly sorry. But it happened before I knew him."

David didn't say anything, so I said "He – well, he doesn't really mean to be vicious. To him, it is just a business – perfectly impersonal."

David let go of my hands and lit a cigarette, and his hands were trembling. "Some business!" he said, his lips tight.

To change the subject, after several moments of uncomfortable silence, I asked, "Is Mrs. Whitmore seriously ill?"

He nodded. "Yes. She – well, she'll never have to stand trial for anything. That's one blessing." He patted my knee, stood up and said, "Come on; let's go over and see her. She may not have much time left."

He went out into the hall and toward the back of the house, and I heard him say, "Mary, we're going over to the hospital. We'll be back in a little while."

Mary asked, "Is Miss Grayson coming back for dinner?"

David said, "Yes, she'll be back. Fix the guest room for her. She'll be staying here, as long as we have you here to chaperone us."

I went out into the hall just as David was closing the door to the kitchen. "What makes you so sure?" I asked.

He came and put an arm around my shoulders. "Because I am going to make sure you do," he said. "You're not going to get away from me ever again." He leaned down and kissed me on the forehead.

As we were driving to the hospital in his station wagon, I said, "There are some things I still don't understand."

"What?"

"I don't understand where you fit into the picture in the Whitmore mess. Why did Mary call you the night before last?"

For a moment he didn't answer; then he said, "Well, Mrs. Whitmore is my great-aunt. My grandmother was a Phipps. I never knew Aunt Agnes very well, but last year when I was traveling through the South Pacific looking for background material for a couple of books, I met her accidentally in the Kroon country. She seemed glad to see me, and I got the impression she wasn't too happy, and was frightened. I questioned her, but she wouldn't tell me anything. Then, shortly after I left, Warren died. He was supposed to have had a heart attack, but I've always had my suspicions. He wasn't at all liked by the natives who worked for him.

"Then I heard Aunt Agnes had come back to the United States, and Coral had come with her. This worried me, because I knew she and Coral didn't get along, and Coral was not the kind of girl who would have accompanied her step-grandmother back to the States out of the goodness of her heart. She was up to something, that I was sure of.

"I had two books to write, already contracted for, and I was behind schedule, so I decided that Sand's End would be a good place for me to hole in for a few months. I'd seen it once when I was a kid when I'd been here with my father and mother and sister, and remembered it as a quiet, isolated spot – the kind I needed to work in until I finished my two books. And if I was up here I could keep an eye on Aunt Agnes – just in case she needed me.

"I called her and asked her if I could come up. She seemed glad to have me, so I put my typewriter and a few clothes, some food and a supply of paper into the station wagon and came up.

"But I hadn't figured on Coral. She latched onto me like a leech, and I had a hard time making her understand that I just wasn't interested."

"Did you know she was playing around with Saban?"

"I didn't even know Saban had come over with them until I got up here. Nor did I know about the birds. I knew Aunt Agnes had become very interested in ornithology, and had worked with her husband over in New Guinea and gladly financed their expeditions to the point of nearly impoverishing herself. I guess she wanted the insurance money to buy an aviary down in Florida where she could take the birds for the winter.

"Also, I knew about Warren's collection of precious stones. When he died they found he hadn't left a will, so Aunt Agnes just appropriated the uncut stones and the jewelry and brought them home with her, smuggling them into the country so she wouldn't have to pay duty on them. She admitted that to me one time, chuckling about it."

"How did she do it?"

"I don't know. She wouldn't tell me, and I didn't want to know. It was her business.

But I did know that Coral and her father felt they should have the jewels by right of blood inheritance. And I was sure they would put up a fight for them. That was why I didn't like it when I heard Coral had come over to the States with her step-grandmother."

"Why didn't Mrs. Whitmore keep the stones and jewelry in a safe deposit box at the bank?"

"Your guess is as good as mine on that one."

"When you were staying at the shack out at Sand's End, did you see or hear anything strange?"

"No. But Isaac wasn't here then. He just came over from New Guinea recently."

"And that is why Mrs. Whitmore began to hide her jewelry and the uncut stones? Because she knew Isaac was after them?"

"Yes. But even before that, she realized Coral was stealing things, bit by bit."

"That was why Coral came out to my beach that night, I suppose. She had a metal box buried in the sand by the outhouse. It must have been where she was hiding the stolen jewelry, and she came out to get it before leaving for Boston. And because of Coral's thefts, even before Isaac's arrival, your aunt had conceived the idea of tying bits of blue to the things she still had and leaving them where the bowerbird could find them and weave them into his bower."

"Yes. And I should have guessed what she was doing."

"But you didn't know the bowerbird did that."

"Not until you told me. The bowerbird was just another bird to me. When I was over in the South Pacific, I was more interested in the locale and the people than the birds. As a matter of fact, I didn't bother about the birds at all, except to notice there were some pretty ones flying around."

"I wonder how Isaac knew enough to look for the stones in the bowerbird's bower?"

"Well, at least he knew their habits. And so did Saban. Saban may have caught on to what Aunt Agnes was doing.

"And when she discovered Isaac was over in one of the fishermen's shacks, she got scared. She knew he was ruthless, unscrupulous and would stop at nothing to get what he wanted. And when you told about the masks, she knew he must be in the neighborhood and went looking for him. Whenever they were back here in Pine Grove Harbor, he used to go over there and hobnob with the fishermen. So she guessed he might be there."

I sighed. "What a lot of bother, and loss of life, just for some jewelry."

David smiled and raised an eyebrow. "Jewelry and a cache of uncut precious stones mean money. And lots of people like money."

"I like money, too, but not that much. It's easier to work for it."

He laughed. "That's the way I've always felt about it. Dad's always had plenty – he's a banker out in the middle West – but I always preferred to make my own."

"What will happen to Saban?"

"They may just deport him. He's not a U.S. citizen."

"One thing more. That night when Coral was supposed to have gone down to Boston, did she know her father was living in one of the fishermen's shacks on the other side of the rocks?"

"I doubt it. From what I saw when I met them over in the South Pacific, I got the impression that they all hated each other quite openly."

"Did you meet Coral's mother?"

"Once. She was a pretty native girl. She spoke good English, and she was out to get hers, like the rest of them."

"Is she over here, too?"

"I wouldn't know."

"Could it have been she who phoned you and Mrs. Whitmore, supposedly from Boston, that morning I found Coral?"

He thought about that for a moment. "It could have been, if she's over here. She and Coral had the same sort of English accent. And I don't think Coral and her mother had too much love for one another."

"Then Isaac must have known she was here, and after he'd killed Coral – by mistake – he could have put her up to phoning you and Mrs. Whitmore and pretending she was Coral, so no one would be looking for Coral for a while." I sat thinking for a moment; then something occurred to me. "But how would he have known she was on her way to Boston, if he killed her, thinking she was me?"

David gave me a quick look. "That makes it worse," he said grimly.

"How so?"

"He must have met Coral on the beach, talked to her and found out she was on her way to Boston and had a lot of the jewels with her. Maybe he quarreled with her over them and killed her in cold blood. Or anger."

"That, or Saban could have told him."

David shrugged, and I shuddered. "Poor Mrs. Whitmore," I said. "What a mess she got herself into when she married the attractive stranger just passing through town."

"That's one way of looking at it," David said.

He drove the station wagon into the parking lot back of the hospital and turned off the ignition. I asked, "If Mrs. Whitmore dies, who will get the jewelry? You? Or Coral's mother?"

"I don't know. But I'm sure I don't want it – or the birds." He turned and smiled at me. "But none of that is important. What I want to know now is whether or not you are going to marry me."

I smiled at him and moved closer, kissing his cheek. "Of course I am. Both of you, David Carter and Peter Lindy. Any more foolish questions?"

He put an arm around me and gave me a hug. "Not at the moment," he said.